Claire's Regrettable Outcome

(Rejected Mail-Order Brides)

BOOK 2

By

Cheryl Wright

Copyright

Claire's Regrettable Outcome
(Book 2 - Rejected Mail-Order Brides)
This is book two of a multi-author series, and is completely standalone

Copyright ©2024 by Cheryl Wright

Small Town Romance Publications
ALL RIGHTS RESERVED

Editing: Sarah Lamb

Dedication

To Margaret Tanner, my very dear friend and fellow author, for her enduring encouragement and friendship.

To Alan, my husband of over forty-nine years, who has been a relentless supporter of my writing and dreams for many years.

To You, my wonderful readers, who encourage me to continue writing these stories. It is such a joy knowing so many of you enjoy reading my stories as much as I love writing them for you.

Table of Contents

Chapter One

Bingarly, Montana – 1880s

Claire Foggarty braced herself.

She closed her eyes, breathed deeply, opened her eyes again, then slowly breathed out. Trying to avoid the inevitable, that's what she was doing. Glancing at the two men opposite, she clasped her hands in front of herself, then looked down.

Her heart pounded—Claire had never seen a dead body before.

Earl Morgan, the man who had promised to marry her, lay on the undertaker's slab in front of her.

She cleared her throat. "You're certain this is Earl Morgan?" she asked, hoping a mistake had been made.

"I'm sorry, Miss Foggarty, but this is definitely Earl." The man who identified himself as Deputy Brody Wilson was the one who'd brought Claire here.

It was her own fault—Claire refused to believe the man who had offered via correspondence to marry her was dead. She had cringed at the thought of being a mail-order bride, but what else was she to do? "Well, that's that, I suppose," she said, sounding far more confident than she felt.

The undertaker pulled up the white sheet and covered her betrothed. Covering Earl's face didn't help her situation, but at least she was no longer drawn to the vision before her.

Deputy Wilson came around to her side of the table. "We should leave," he said, and led her out onto the street and into the welcomed fresh air. Claire took several deep breaths, trying to rid herself of the overwhelming stench of death.

Staggering to a nearby wooden bench, she sat contemplating her next move. Now that her plan had gone awry, Claire didn't know what she would do. But she needed to think quickly. It wasn't safe for her to stay in one place for too long.

"What are your plans now?" The deputy's voice cut through her scattered thoughts. Indeed, what would she do? Her only hope was to keep running. "Earl always found himself in the midst of trouble," he added, his voice unsteady.

Claire turned to face him. Why did the death of Earl Morgan affect him so much? "Is that so?" she said, not willing to reveal her thoughts to this stranger. He might be a deputy, but that didn't guarantee the man was honest. "You knew him?"

Brody Wilson leaned back on the hard wooden bench, then moments later leaned forward, putting his head in his hands. "Earl was my cousin," he said, his voice full of emotion. "Deep down he was a good person, but he ran with the wrong crowd."

Trying to take it all in, Claire sat quietly. What if Earl wasn't dead? Would she have been caught up in his dangerous world? She had enough problems of her own. She didn't need to land in even more hot water.

Without warning, Brody reached across and clasped her hands. "As he lay dying, blood pouring from his chest, Earl made me promise…" His voice wavered again, and he seemed to brace himself for the words that were to come. He studied Claire's face, then stared at their still clasped hands. "He made me promise to look after you, and I agreed. So, Claire Foggerty, will you marry me?" he asked, as he dropped to one knee.

Standing abruptly, Claire tried to flee. The deputy clutched her wrist before she could leave. Her mind in a whirl, Claire wasn't sure what to think. Perhaps it was all a joke. Or a nightmare. That must be it— not only was her lifeline to freedom dead, but Earl's cousin was playing with her mind.

Who in their right mind would offer to marry someone they met only minutes before? She put it down to the fact Deputy Brody Wilson was in mourning. The death of a family member could play with your mind. She knew that from experience. When Grandmother passed on, Claire was certain she wouldn't survive the grief. And she probably wouldn't have if she didn't have Grandmother's journal to read.

Except that's where all her troubles began.

The expression on Claire's face told Brody all he needed to know. She was not interested in marrying a lowly deputy.

Instead of disclosing his true identity, Earl had told her he was a bank manager. If it hadn't been so deceitful, it would be laughable. He might have worked in the bank at one time, but as janitor, he wasn't even close to being the bank manager.

Brody preferred to describe his cousin as a rambler, rather than the hired gun he'd become famous for. Earl was good, but not good enough. His last job was the one that killed him. Why anyone would go after Wild John Hickory, he would never know. Hickory was the most experienced gun for hire not only in the county, but in the whole of Montana.

"Miss Foggarty," Brody said, still gripping her wrist. "I'm only trying to do right by you. It's what Earl wanted."

She shook her head and tried to pull out of his grip. "I…" She closed her eyes, and Brody was certain she was weighing up her options. "I need to think about it," she finally said. Brody was certain it was a veiled attempt at refusing his proposal without actually saying so.

At his insistence, she sat on the wooden bench again. "Can we at least talk about it? What will you do now? Where will you go?" He was certain she wouldn't have a Plan B since she'd expected to be married by now. Brody glanced at his pocket watch, then studied his companion. Her tight lips told him all he needed to know—she was not impressed with the situation she found herself in. Brody could only imagine what was going through her mind.

She turned to face him. "I have no idea what I'll do. Except I can't stay here." Claire turned away and glanced at the large bag she carried, then clutched it tightly.

His eyes focused on that bag. Most women did not carry such large bags with them. Where was her reticule? Did she arrive with no belongings? The situation became more and more intriguing by the minute. "My stomach is telling me it's time to eat. Will you join me? We can discuss the situation further."

As if on cue, her stomach rumbled, and Miss Foggarty appeared devastated. "My apologies," she said quietly.

Brody frowned. "When did you last eat?" he demanded. Without waiting for an answer, he dragged Claire to her feet and pulled her toward the diner.

"I…I have no money," she admitted, her voice so low he barely heard her speak.

He stopped where they stood in the middle of the main road, causing her to trip. Brody stopped her fall by pulling her close. He wasn't adverse to her soft, pliable body. The moment the thought entered his mind, he knew he needed to expel it. "Even more reason for you to marry me," he said firmly.

He opened the door to the diner, his heart pounding so loud he could barely hear himself think.

Brody seated Claire, then sat opposite her. He already knew she had to be desperate to become a mail-order bride. Otherwise, why would she risk traveling to a strange place to marry a man she'd never met? "Let me tell you about my cousin—the man you were to marry."

He stared across the table at her, and she squirmed under his gaze. "I know enough. He told me in a letter." She smiled briefly, and Brody knew it was forced.

His eyebrows lifted in question. Did she really know the man she was to marry, or did she only think she did? He was certain it was the latter. "What do you think happened to Earl?" he asked firmly. He didn't want to shock her, and he didn't particularly want to marry her either, but it was becoming clear he needed to do both.

She blinked a few times, then shook her head. "I don't know what happened to him. Why would anyone kill the bank manager, unless it was a robbery?" She stared at him.

"It wasn't a robbery, and he wasn't the bank manager." Now that he'd said it, Brody wanted to take back the words. The last thing he wanted was to tarnish his cousin's memory, but she would surely find out soon enough. Anyone in town could give her the same information.

All color drained from her face at his words.

Moments later, the waitress brought menus for them. It was a welcomed interruption. Claire glanced up at the waitress. "Thank you," she said quietly.

Brody knew he'd shocked her, but the truth had to be told. She needed to understand she'd avoided a catastrophe. "The chicken pot pie is really good," Brody told her. "Along with the steak." Not that he could really afford the steak, not on a deputy's wage. In a matter of days, he would be sheriff, which would make it easier. Sheriff Dodd had announced his retirement, and Brody was confirmed as his replacement.

As deputy, he wasn't paid as much as the sheriff, and didn't get the extra benefits. The best of those benefits being the sheriff's accommodation at no charge to him. On the other hand, the sheriff's deputy didn't take the same risks.

"Why would Earl tell me he was the bank manager if he wasn't?" Claire asked, her words unsure. Sadness crossed her face. "I was a fool to accept him at his word, wasn't I?"

Brody wanted to say she was, but she'd had enough bad news for one day. "Not at all. You weren't to know Earl wasn't who he said he was." If his cousin was still alive, he would ring his scrawny neck for lying to this vulnerable woman. He'd mentioned he wanted a wife, and Brody did his best to talk Earl out of it. With his lifestyle, how did Earl expect to have a wife and family? It was a fool's errand.

Before he had the opportunity to answer, their waitress was back to take their orders. "We need to talk," Brody said, repeating what he'd said earlier. "Not here, though. It's too busy right now." He glanced about the diner. It wasn't full, but several diners were in close proximity. It wasn't long and their food was placed in front of them. Claire leaned forward and breathed in the aroma.

"It smells delicious," she said, then picked up her cutlery. Brody watched as she ate—it was clear she hadn't eaten for days. Not that she'd confessed that fact. She was like a starving street urchin, and it broke his heart. What made her come out west to marry a complete stranger? No decent woman would uproot themselves to do so unless there was a very good reason.

He was more than a little interested to find out what forced her to run.

"Joshua Foggarty was the man of my heart. From the moment our eyes met across the dance floor, I knew we would be together for the rest of our lives."

The more Claire learned about Earl Morgan, the more she realized she'd avoided disaster. She had enough problems of her own, without having to worry about having married a man who was a compulsive liar. Although that might be an unfair assumption since the man was dead.

She was now certain he believed she wouldn't travel to this small town if she knew what Earl really did for a living.

"Oh," Claire said out of the blue. "You didn't tell me what your cousin did do for a living." She felt herself stiffen, wondering what she was about to be told. Everything had gone so wrong today that nothing would surprise her.

Brody put down his knife and fork, and reached for her hand. "I don't think you want to know," he said gently as he caressed her hand.

Claire blinked rapidly. How bad could it be? "I most certainly do want to know," she said forcefully. "I believe I have a right to know what I may have gotten myself into." She pursed her lips to show him she meant business.

Instead of telling her, he chuckled. Did the deputy believe it was all some big joke? It certainly wasn't to Claire. She pulled her hand out of his grasp. "I'm waiting," she said firmly, and his smile disappeared.

"My cousin Earl, your betrothed, was a gun for hire."

"He…he was a gunslinger? I was going to marry a killer?" Claire felt the color drain from her face. Her mouth was dry, and her appetite was suddenly gone.

It was no wonder Earl told her he was the bank manager. Despite her situation, she would not have agreed to marry Earl Morgan had she known he was a hired killer. Why would someone like that even want to marry? It was beyond comprehension.

Claire shook her head. Brody pushed a glass of water toward her. "I'm sorry," he said, sounding as though he truly meant it. "Now you know why I didn't want to tell you."

She glanced up into the deputy's face. He did appear apologetic, although it wasn't his fault. As a man of the law, he likely despised his cousin's chosen occupation. If you could call it that. Claire reached for the water and took two large gulps of it. Then choked on it. Brody hurried around to her and pounded her back until she stopped coughing. She glanced up into his face. Deputy Brody Wilson had kind eyes. He seemed to be a kind man.

Perhaps she should marry him after all?

The moment Claire had agreed to marry Brody, he started making arrangements. First item on his agenda was to spoil her with a bubble bath. For Claire, though, she needed clothes. Having to run for her life meant leaving everything behind. Her façade of being calm and collected was only skin deep. How she wasn't totally disheveled, Claire had no idea.

Brody took her to the mercantile where she chose two gowns and undergarments. That would get her through their wedding and keep her clothed for a few days. Not once did he question the fact she'd arrived with nothing.

Perhaps if she'd had more time to find out about Earl, she wouldn't be standing here right now. Nor would she be destitute. The bridal agency handed her a letter and she accepted the first one given to her. They immediately sent a telegraph to let Claire's groom know she would arriving in three days' time.

It was a far cry from the love match her grandparents had enjoyed.

How did one go from being an heiress with the world at her fingertips to having nothing, not even a dollar to her name? Not to mention running for her life.

Claire straightened her back. There was no time for self-pity. Brody was keen to marry her, and it was crystal clear he wanted it to happen this very day. It made Claire suspicious. Was there something about him she needed to know? Perhaps it was all a façade and deep down he was a nasty, vicious, creature.

She shuddered at the thought.

Before she could ponder the issue further, Brody took her to the bath house. That was an experience all of its own.

Never before had she undressed in front of strangers. Nor had she bathed with other women. It was certainly a shock to the system, and Claire wasn't convinced she would recover. Her husband-to-be had no idea of her background, nor did she intend to tell him.

After soaking for as short a time as possible to ensure she was clean, despite sharing the water with several other women, Claire felt better. She did wonder if it was commonplace to have shared baths, or whether she was unlucky and it was the practice in this particular town.

Nonetheless, she needed to move forward. She hurriedly dried herself, then dressed ready to marry her betrothed's cousin. Claire still couldn't believe the way the day had unfolded and hoped there were no more unwelcomed surprises.

As she stood in front of the preacher, Brody by her side, Claire was dazed. Brody insisted they marry immediately. At her own admission, Claire was penniless. At least now she was. Less than a week ago she was an heiress, in line for a fortune.

As she'd continued reading her grandmother's journal, Claire realized her situation was now precarious. In the beginning, it was simply a beautiful love story. One she would never forget.

She recalled the beautifully crafted words in her grandmother's hand. They had melted Claire's heart as she read them. Who wouldn't fall to pieces reading the words of a woman falling in love? It was far better than reading one of those dime romance novels, because she knew this story was true.

Every day Claire sat in the window seat of the family home reading more of Clarissa Foggarty's journal. She learned far more about her grandparents than she ever believed possible. Grandfather had died before Claire was born, and she reveled in learning about him too.

Brody nudging her in the ribs brought Claire out of her thoughts. "I… I do," she said, not certain that was even what was expected of her.

"I now pronounce you man and wife," the preacher told them.

Claire was heartbroken. Her grandparents and her parents had traditional weddings. One with all the grandeur and ceremony befitting the Foggarty family. It was expected that Claire would do the same. How could she do that when she was on the run?

Her hope now was that changing her surname would keep her safe. The last thing she wanted to do was pull this dear man into her ring of danger. At least as a lawman he would be able to protect her, but would he be able to protect himself?

Therein was the problem.

Chapter Four

Brody's heart pounded. Had he really just married this complete stranger? Despite what he'd promised his cousin, he still had reservations.

It was too late for that now.

As they walked back down the aisle to the outside world, he pondered the days ahead. As they stood on the steps leading into the church, Brody noticed the sadness that filled his bride's expression. "Is everything alright?" he asked, quietly knowing it must be a far cry from what she'd expected for her wedding day.

She shook her head gently. "It's nothing." She blinked a few times before continuing. "I guess I expected a bit more fanfare. Marrying a bank manager." She shrugged her shoulders, and Claire's disappointment hit him harder than he'd imagined. "I've survived worse," she said. Brody thought it a strange thing for his bride to say.

Grasping the paper bag that held her new clothes, her worldly goods, Brody faced her. "I haven't been completely honest with you," he said. She scowled. "I can't move into the sheriff's place until the current sheriff moves out." This time she frowned.

"What does that mean?" Claire asked.

"I'll have to put you up in the women's boarding house." He pointed to a small building further up the road. "I live in the men's boarding house—no women allowed."

Her shoulders sagged. His bride's disappointment was evident. Whether it was because she didn't want to be alone on their wedding night, or wanted to start afresh, he wasn't sure. But something seemed to be on her mind. Whether she would confess to him, Brody doubted. He would have to win her trust before that could happen.

"I'll pay, so don't worry about that." She looked relieved, which left Brody believing money had been her concern. They headed toward the women's boarding house, both seemingly feeling the same way—disconcerted at the way things had turned out. Claire appeared disgruntled, and Brody felt frustrated at having to be separated from his new wife.

It made him wonder what her life would have been like had she married Earl. His cousin was not only a gunslinger, but a rebel. Earl did what Earl wanted to do, not what society demanded. He was never imprisoned as the law could never prove his hand in any of the killings he was involved with. Of course, he boasted to his deputy cousin, knowing Brody couldn't act on the information. Hearsay was not acceptable in a court of law, and Earl knew it.

As much as Brody was sad his cousin was dead, he wasn't upset his murdering days were over. There had been some instances of mistaken identity, he was certain. Unexplained deaths of totally innocent citizens did not sit well with Brody.

Once the funeral was over, he could get on with his life. His new life as sheriff, and a married man. The latter worried him far more than becoming Bingarli's sheriff, and he would be the first to admit it.

"Here were are," he said, standing outside the boarding house with Claire. "Mrs. Goodall will look after you."

"Couldn't we stay at the hotel?" Claire asked before they took another step.

"I'm not the sheriff yet," Brody said firmly. "Besides, I'm already paying for my accommodation, so that would be doubling up." Did that sound harsh? Or perhaps he sounded mean? "I…I'm not a miser," he said quickly. "The truth is, I wasn't expecting to get married today." His words all seemed muddled, and Brody was dismayed. What was wrong with him? He never fumbled over his words like this. Still, it had been a difficult day. Earl had died earlier in the day, and by afternoon Brody was married in his place.

Claire studied him. "I never asked—when did Earl pass?" She licked her lips as though it was a life and death answer for her. Which seemed rather strange. Still, she had a right to know.

"This morning. Quite early, in fact. He'd been making plans for your marriage when he was shot." Brody's voice broke on the last words. As much as Earl was a killer for hire, he was a family member, and one who was dearly loved. Even despite his dreadful occupation.

Claire reached out and touched his shoulder. "I'm sorry. I didn't know."

"Of course you didn't. Nothing you did would have stopped this happening. He has been dodging bullets for a long time now."

Nodding her head, Claire seemed to understand, but did she really? What she truly needed to understand was *she* had dodged a bullet. Who knew if she could have taken a bullet in Earl's place as retaliation. Brody didn't even want to think about it.

He went up the few steps to the front door and knocked. Unlike the men's boarding house, Mrs. Goodall had prettied the place up. Out the front was a white picket fence and a small garden of various colored flowers. Lacy curtains hung on each of the front windows, giving the place an almost fairytale look. He turned to his bride. "You should be comfortable here. It's only for a few days, then we can move into the sheriff's cottage."

Before she had a chance to answer, the door opened. Mrs. Goodall stood before them, a scowl on her face. "Deputy," she said, her tone harsh. Brody didn't blame her—the last time he'd visited, it was to arrest one of her boarders for stealing from the mercantile.

"Mrs. Goodall," he said as pleasantly as he could muster. "I've brought my bride, Claire Fog…" He'd almost used her maiden name. "Claire Wilson," he corrected. "I don't have access to the sheriff's cottage until Sheriff Dodd moves out later this week."

"Mrs. Wilson," she said pleasantly, turning to face Claire. "You're in luck. I have one room available, and it happens to be the best one in the place." She reached for Claire's hand, totally ignoring Brody, and showed her inside. "Take a seat," he heard the woman say, then she returned to Brody, her hand outreached. He reached into his pocket and placed the coins in her hand. "Is that your wife's belongings?" Mrs. Goodall asked. "It's not much."

"Her luggage was lost in transit," he said, handing her the paper carry bag. Brody had no idea why Claire had no luggage, and given the circumstances didn't think to ask. "I'll replenish her clothes once we're in our new home."

Not saying another word, Mrs. Goodall closed the door in his face. Brody felt lost. He had no idea why.

He'd been married to Claire for less than an hour, and already he missed her. Right now, he wished Sheriff Dodd would leave early and hand the cottage over to Brody. Except he knew that wouldn't happen.

Besides, he'd already paid for his accommodation for the duration, as well as Claire's. He might as well go back to the sheriff's office and complete some paperwork.

"As he held me close, I knew, had my father been there at the dance, he would have intervened. As handsome as he was, I immediately knew Joshua Foggarty was trouble."

Claire sat on the edge of the comfortable chair in the sitting room. Her nerves were getting the better of her. The plan was always she would marry the day she arrived, but not to this man. Not to Brody Wilson, deputy soon to be sheriff.

She should be grateful she wasn't married to a killer. Had she known, Claire would never have accepted Earl's proposal. Thankfully, it had turned out for the better. At least she hoped it had.

"How are you doing, dear?" Mrs. Goodall's voice brought Claire out of her thoughts. "It can't be easy being separated from your new husband."

Claire glanced up at the boarding house owner. "It's truly not," she said quietly. She gave no clue her reason for feeling that way was not what the other woman believed. Changing her name might help keep her safe, but there was absolutely no guarantee it was the case.

Mrs. Goodall sat down next to her and reached for Claire's hand. "You seem like the type to make the best of whatever is placed in front of you." She squeezed Claire's hand. "Sheriff Dodd will vacate the cottage soon. Then you'll begin your new life with Deputy Wilson."

Having a new name as well as a completely new location was what Claire needed. But would it be enough? She was vulnerable to whoever was chasing her, even if Claire had no idea what it was all about.

Reaching for her oversized bag, Claire tapped it to assure herself the journal was still there. It wasn't like she could have lost it between here and the church—it had been in her possession the entire time.

Glancing at the older woman again, Claire had to ask. "You don't seem to like Deputy Wilson. Er, my husband," she said warily. "Might I ask why?"

Mrs. Goodall's face tightened. "He arrested one of my boarders," she said flatly, then waved a hand about. "I know the girl had stolen from the mercantile, but he surely could have arrested her elsewhere."

Pondering the situation, Claire wondered if that wasn't so bad. "He was probably only doing his job," she finally said.

Mrs. Goodall stood. "I'm certain you're right, dear. Besides, he has to do what the sheriff tells him." She wiped her hands on her apron. "A cup of tea would be nice, I think. How do you have yours?" she asked as she reached up to pull down two mugs.

"That sounds wonderful. Milk and no sugar, thank you," Claire said, finally feeling more relaxed.

It wasn't long before a mug of hot tea sat in front of her, along with a plate of assorted muffins. She reached for one and discovered it was still warm. Claire took a bite. It was even more delicious than the muffins Cook made back home.

The thought sent her mind reeling. Her family must be worried about her—she'd left without a word, knowing they would convince her to stay if she told them she had to leave. Now, though, she couldn't let them know where she was, or why.

Whoever was after her would then be able to follow the trail, and no doubt, find her.

Her feet felt for the bag that held the journal. She had no idea what was in the journal that caused the problem, but something in her grandmother's journal put her life in danger. Perhaps she should simply hand it over to the sheriff and let him deal with it.

Although she was married to the deputy who was about to become sheriff, Claire wasn't certain she wanted to tell her husband she had put him in danger, too.

Did that mean the citizens of Bingarli were in jeopardy? It was all Claire could do not to cry in despair.

Mrs. Goodall reached across the table, and covered Claire's hand with her own. "I know your situation is a difficult one," she said gently, "but in a few days, everything will turn out fine. You mark my words." She handed Claire a handkerchief. It was then she realized tears slipped down her cheeks.

"I'm so sorry," Claire told her hostess. "It's been a difficult few days. Being relegated here was the last straw." She wiped her eyes, then reached for her mug and sipped the hot tea. Her tears were relentless and Claire could barely see the other woman. Despite that, she'd already learned Mrs. Goodall was a kind and caring woman. "I arrived this morning, prepared to marry my groom, only to find him dead!" She blurted out the last words, not thinking about whether they would be repeated. Was Mrs. Goodall the town gossip? Claire hoped not.

"My dear girl, were you to marry Earl?" She shook her head sadly. "A lost cause, that one. You are far better off with Deputy Wilson." Mrs. Goodall patted Claire's hand. "Don't worry—I won't tell a soul."

"Thank you," Claire said between sips of tea. "I'm sure the deputy wouldn't be happy with me sharing those details."

Mrs. Goodall waved a hand across in front of herself. "That Earl Morgan was always trouble. Everyone in town knew his life would be short. Still, he was around far longer than most of us predicted." She shook her head sadly. "May he rest in peace," she added quietly.

Claire wasn't sure what to say. Apparently, the entire town knew he was a killer, and yet Earl walked the streets a free man. She swiped at her stray tears. "How was he not in jail? Please don't tell me it was my husband's doing."

"I might have my disagreements with the deputy, but no. It wasn't his fault. Unfortunately, Earl was far too good at what he did. As hard as the sheriff and deputy tried, there was never proof that Earl Morgan was the murderer in any of the cases." Mrs. Goodall sighed then. "When he wasn't trying to kill someone, Earl was the nicest young man. It is such a pity."

Claire's heart thudded. She really had dodged a bullet. She had enough troubles of her own without finding herself in more hot water with a killer for a husband. Claire didn't want to think badly of Earl— after all the man was dead. She'd seen the proof of that herself. The thought churned her stomach.

She'd felt as though Brody had dumped her at the boarding house, like he was disposing of rubbish. Only now she understood more about his predicament. He was in a similar situation to Claire. He'd found himself in the middle of things, just as she had.

If Claire had arrived one day earlier, perhaps even a few hours earlier, she may have been married to the hired gun. Where would that have left her? If she thought her position was difficult now, she would have had far fewer choices had she married the man, then he was killed.

What if he'd been killed as they left the church? Claire wondered if she would still be alive now. Mrs. Goodall was right—she had certainly been lucky arriving when she did.

"I think a change of scenery is in order," Mrs. Goodall told her. "Let me show you to your room." She turned to face Claire. "It's the biggest and prettiest room of them all. I'm so glad it was available for you, my dear. I think it will cheer you up." She smiled and Claire felt joy for the first time today.

She hoped it was the beginning of happiness, and the end of the dismay she'd suffered.

Chapter Six

Brody sat at his desk shuffling papers. He was far too distracted to actually fill out the forms.

"What on earth is wrong with you, Brody?" Sheriff Dodd asked. "You are usually efficient with your time."

Glancing up at the sheriff, Brody supposed he should tell the retiring sheriff his news. "I got married today," he said, then went back to shuffling papers around his desk.

"You what? Are you crazy? Besides, I didn't know you were seeing anyone." He studied Brody to the point he almost squirmed under the sheriff's gaze.

"Earl's mail-order bride," he mumbled. "Earl made me promise I'd marry her."

"Of course he did, but he wouldn't have known otherwise. Your murdering cousin is dead."

Sheriff Dodd had never minced words when it came to Earl, and he certainly wasn't doing it now. "I promised Earl I would. Besides, it's too late—we're already married." This time, he picked up a pencil and began filling out the forms.

"So, where is this bride of yours?"

"At the boarding house." Even to his own ears, Brody sounded defeated. "I had no choice." He glanced up at his boss.

"Brody," Sheriff Dodd said firmly, "I have vacated the sheriff's residence. I moved out over the weekend. It's yours to do whatever you wish." He walked over and patted the younger man's shoulder. "I wish you both all the best, despite the rocky start."

His heart hammered in his chest. What was he meant to do now? He'd paid for Claire's accommodation, as well as his own. Brody had no doubt he would not get a refund. Still, he knew his bride was upset at being separated from him. Especially given she knew absolutely no one in town except him. Unless you counted the undertaker and preacher.

By now, Mrs. Goodall would probably have told her what a terrible person he was. Brody was only doing his job. He wasn't sure what else she expected him to do. Until that episode, Mrs. Goodall had treated him fairly. Now the older woman held it against him, and probably would for the rest of her days.

"Here, take these. Prepare for your bride." Sheriff Dodd handed him a set of keys. "It's clean and tidy, but you might want to make a few changes. Make it your own. The missus might want to add curtains— you know what women are like." He rolled his eyes then. "Or perhaps you don't. Why don't you fetch her and show her the place. Then you two can spend the next few days fixing the place up to suit you both." He walked out then, and didn't look back.

They had no prisoners right now, so Brody left the sheriff's office and went next door to the residence. It was a stroke of luck the sheriff had already moved out. How did he not know? Brody shook his head, then unlocked the front door. It smelled clean and fresh. Not that he'd expected much else. Bingarli was a relatively new town. Both he and Sheriff Dodd had been recruited from their positions at the time to come here and ensure the town was a law abiding one. It had been purpose built, which he'd thought rather strange, but people were flocking to newer towns. Especially those that were not overrun by outlaws and criminals.

Only a few years old, this town was built specifically to fill the gap between neighboring towns. It had helped the town to prosper. He enjoyed being there, and hoped his new bride did too. Whatever she needed, Claire should be able to buy in town. If it wasn't available, they could order in.

It was then he realized he knew absolutely nothing about Claire Foggerty. Er, Wilson. Now they had a home of their own, they could get it set up to suit themselves, and then they would talk. Brody wanted to know everything about his bride.

He only hoped she wanted to tell him. Being a mail-order bride, was she running away? If so, what was she running from? His curiosity getting the better of him, Brody stepped into the sheriff's residence. He needed to take his mind off problems that might not even exist.

~*~

"I have a surprise for you," Brody said as he sat opposite his new bride. He had denied Mrs. Goodall's offer of refreshments. She'd only offered out of politeness he was certain.

Claire's sad expression changed in an instant. "What is it?" she asked excitedly. He noticed Mrs. Goodall's smile out the corner of his eye.

"If I told you, it wouldn't be a surprise." Brody reached for her hands and pulled Claire to her feet. "You need to come with me."

He led her to the front door, then headed toward their new home. Well, it would be once it was fixed up the way Claire wanted.

Once outside, he hooked her arm through his. "It doesn't take long to get there," he said, his excitement building. Brody couldn't believe how much he was looking forward to showing his bride their new home. It was but a shell right now, but once she put her stamp on it, their little cottage would become a home.

Brody suddenly felt nervous. What if Claire hated it? What would they do then? The sheriff's residence was part of his salary package. It would save a big chunk of money each month. As they almost reached their destination, Brody stumbled. He only hoped she liked it.

"Where are we?" Claire asked as Brody began to unlock the door. He kicked it open, then lifted his bride into his arms and carried her across the threshold. He stared down into her face. He'd been mourning the loss of his cousin when they met, and hadn't really taken in her appearance.

His bride was beautiful. Except right now she looked far more concerned than he wished for her. "This is the sheriff's cottage," he said as they stepped inside. "Sheriff Dodd gave me the keys a short time ago."

Claire studied him. "He's already moved out?" A slow smile came to her face. Brody couldn't know if that was because she wanted to be with him, or because she would have a base.

"He left early. I only just found out." He carefully set his bride on her feet. "It's furnished, but we will need to get a few supplies."

Without another word, Claire hurried into the kitchen. Brody stood in the doorway watching as she opened each cupboard. At least he wouldn't have to buy kitchen supplies, but he did need to buy staples from the mercantile. "Make a list of the food you need, and we'll visit the mercantile," he said.

His wife stared at him. Then she looked bewildered. "I hope *you* can cook," she said firmly. "Because I certainly can't."

Brody's heart sank. He thought all women could cook. Wasn't that part of their upbringing, to learn how to cook? He stared at her, hoping Claire was joking. Only she wasn't laughing. "You're serious," he finally said.

"We have a cook…" she began, then clammed up. Her cheeks turned a rosy color, and she seemed annoyed with herself for speaking. She studied him, then ran out of the kitchen. He watched as she went from one room to another. Finally, Claire glanced at the windows. "There are no window coverings," she told him, her tone almost accusing.

"I took them down. They were old and torn. I'm not sure why Sheriff Dodd put up with them like that." He studied her. "You can make some more. This way you get to choose the fabric you want." He smiled, but it didn't placate his wife. Tears swam in her eyes. "You can't sew?"

Something was not quite right. Claire was a seemingly intelligent woman who'd signed up as a mail-order bride. She can't cook, nor can she sew. Both were requirements of becoming a mail-order bride. At least Brody assumed they were.

He didn't push her for information, but using his skills as a man of the law, Brody knew Claire was hiding something. What that was, he didn't know. Not yet, but he vowed to find out.

He led her into the sitting room and guided her to sit on the sofa. "Is there something you want to tell me?" Brody asked, his eyes never leaving his wife's face.

Claire closed her eyes against his scrutiny.

Chapter Seven

"The more I learn about him, the more I am convinced Joshua is not being honest with me. Father says he's a scoundrel and not to be trusted. I'm beginning to believe him."

Claire sighed. She couldn't keep her eyes closed forever, as much as she wanted to. Brody's gaze made her uncomfortable, and for good reason. She pulled her oversized bag closer and tapped it to assure herself the journal was still there. Not that she had any reason to think it wasn't, but she had to be certain.

Brody moved closer to her, his body snuggling next to hers. She opened her eyes. *That wasn't appropriate!* It was then she remembered she'd married this man, this stranger. At least she knew he was a real person, and wasn't pretending to be someone he wasn't.

Her heart thudded. Not only had her betrothed been killed this very day, but she'd been totally misled about who he was. *A bank manager indeed!*

Her head now pounding, Claire opened her eyes to find Brody still gazing at her. "I...I'm not sure what you mean," she said carefully, and pulled the journal closer still. She should have known better. Brody's eyes immediately went to the bag she protected with her life.

The bag that presumably was the reason her life was in danger. To be honest, she really didn't know why she was being followed. Or why men, dangerous men, had tried to steal the journal. Not only once, but on several occasions.

"Claire," Brody said firmly, startling her. "What's in that bag?" He scowled at her, and Claire cringed, shuffling her way to the end of the sofa.

"It's my grandmother's journal," she said truthfully. "See for yourself." She opened the bag and he peeked inside. There was nothing else in there, and now he saw it with his own eyes.

"Then why do you covet the bag if it's only a journal?" His suspicious expression told Claire he didn't believe her.

She pulled the journal out of the bag, but not before glancing out of the window to ensure no one was watching. Surely they hadn't followed her here? Bingarli was but a pinprick on the map.

When her attention came back to Brody, he was studying her. Closely. He reached for the bag and pulled out the journal. It was old and tattered after all these years. Clarissa Foggarty had written in it religiously, her thoughts laid bare.

"I don't think Grandmother expected anyone to read it," she said, staring down at the journal in her husband's hands. "It's not worth anything, except it's precious to me." Claire felt her emotions growing, and fought back her tears. "More than anything, I've felt comforted by her words." She glanced up at him and studied him the way he had her. "In it, she says my grandfather was a scoundrel."

Brody laughed, and Claire felt relieved. "I'm sorry," he said, sounding every bit as remorseful as Claire wanted to believe he was.

"There is nothing terrible in it—take a look for yourself." She opened at a random page, and they both stared at the words. "What did I tell you? Nearly every entry, my grandmother says what a gentleman my grandfather was, even if she did believe he was hiding something. He died before I was born. The journal means I can learn more about him. And Grandmother Clarissa, too."

When she glanced at Brody again, his eyes were open wide in amazement. "Joshua Foggarty was your grandfather?"

Claire was confused. "You know him? Or should I say *of him*? My grandfather was rich, but I have no idea how he got that way. I always assumed he'd inherited his fortune." Her heart pounding, Claire snatched back the journal that was so precious to her. "I…I want to leave now," she said firmly. She didn't like where this conversation was going.

Brody stared at her. "You haven't told me your opinion of the cottage," Brody said. "Not that it matters. This is where we will be living."

Clutching the bag and the journal close to her chest, Claire headed toward the front door, Brody close on her heels. "If that's the case, why did you bother asking me here?" She huffed then, and headed back toward the boarding house.

It was the last thing she wanted to do, but Brody seemed to know something about Joshua Foggarty. By the sounds of it, it wasn't particularly good.

"Claire, wait," Brody called after her. "I didn't mean to upset you." He reached her far quicker than Claire believed possible. Her husband was tall, far taller than her, and was next to her in record time.

"I don't know anything about your grandfather, but the name is familiar. I can't think why." Only Claire wasn't convinced Brody's words were true. The moment he'd seen her grandfather's name, he'd seemed surprised, shocked even.

He grabbed Claire's arm as she tried to get away. She glared at him. Brody's hands dropped away.

"Just because I am your wife does not give you the right to manhandle me," Claire snapped at him, then turned away. Not only had he denigrated her grandfather's memory, but he seemed to be implying there was more to his story.

"You're right. I'm sorry—I don't know what came over me." Brody was remorseful, that was clear. They were both on edge. Neither expected to marry the other, so it was a shock to them both. "Can we start over?"

Claire stared at him. She took a deep, fortifying breath and let it out slowly. At least here in Bingarli she had the opportunity to do so. Back home, she seemed to always be hiding herself away. "That's a good idea," she said, her voice slightly above a whisper.

Brody led her back inside the cottage. "It's not much, I know," he said. "But it will do. It comes with the job, so it will allow us to build a nest egg."

A nest egg? Was Brody planning on making a future with her? Claire believed this to be more a marriage of convenience. Hadn't he married Earl's bride so she wouldn't be left on her own? At least, that was the way Claire understood it. Either way, it wasn't for love—they had met less than an hour before they stood in front of the preacher and said their marriage vows.

Claire glanced about. Only this time, she took in her surroundings. Previously, she'd been preoccupied with Brody's questions. And his nearness. Propriety was paramount in the Foggarty mansion, but not so much in this outback town. "Does the furniture stay or do we have to start over?" she asked. Claire couldn't recall if she'd asked the question earlier. Brody's questions had sent her off kilter.

"It stays—I told you this earlier. We do need to provide our own sheets and towels. And food, of course." He studied her for long moments, and Claire wondered what he saw. "You really can't cook?"

"I really can't," she whispered. When in her lifetime did anyone believe she would marry a small town deputy, rather than one of the rich heirs who had determined to court her?

Brody slipped an arm around her shoulders and pulled her close. "We'll work it out," he told her, and Claire was certain they would.

Chapter Eight

At the mercantile, Claire chose fabric for window covers. At her own admission, she couldn't sew, which left them with a dilemma.

"I can make them for you," Edna Jackson, the mercantile owner's wife offered. "See it as a wedding gift," she added at Brody's objection.

"Thank you," his new bride said, and Brody smiled. No matter what was going on with her, she was always polite and grateful. It surprised him since she was apparently from a privileged background. The only hint of that came when they discussed her grandmother's journal.

"You don't have to do that, Edna," Brody interjected. "I'm happy to pay."

Edna pulled out a tape measure. "I'm sure I can trust you to measure the windows," she told Brody, ignoring his comment completely. "If you get them to me by tonight, you will have your window coverings to coincide with you both moving in." She was beaming now, and as much as Brody was grateful, he didn't want anyone to feel like they owed him anything.

Brody had the store owner compile a box of kitchen staples they would need for the pantry, along with two sets of sheets, some bedding, and towels. It would be a large bill, but it wasn't like it would be a weekly occurrence. From now on, the groceries would be topped up as they were used, rather than this large order to get them started.

It was somewhat like their marriage.

He didn't regret marrying his cousin's bride. It was more neither of them knew the other. Not that Earl had known her either. He'd received a telegram three days beforehand saying his bride-to-be was in a bad situation and would arrive two days later. Brody shrugged his shoulders. No matter which way he looked at it, Claire was marrying a complete stranger.

At least the stranger she married wasn't a killer for hire.

They left the mercantile with Brody carrying a large box of supplies. Claire ran ahead and unlocked the sheriff's cottage. At first, she seemed apprehensive, and Brody couldn't fathom why. He was acutely aware she didn't want to be in the boarding house. Whether it was because they were separated he wasn't certain.

She'd certainly had a shock that morning, within minutes of her arrival. In hindsight, he should have taken her somewhere private and told her Earl was dead, rather than confronting her with his dead body. He knew now it was a cruel thing to do.

Especially when she had traveled a long way to marry his cousin.

She had demanded proof of Earl's demise, and left him with no choice. Still, guilt filled him at the memory.

Claire held the door open for him as Brody approached. His heart fluttered simply looking at her. This was the furthest from his plans for the day, and he was certain Claire would feel the same. "Shall I put these in the kitchen?" Brody asked as he lingered near that room.

"Oh! Of course," Claire told him. "I hadn't given it a thought."

He placed the heavy box on the kitchen table. At least he didn't have to go out and buy furniture. That would have been pushing his budget a bit. He had some money saved, but didn't want to stretch it to the limit.

Claire set about removing the linen from the box, then put all the food supplies in the pantry. He followed her in, his arms full of supplies. He couldn't help but grin at the haphazard way she filled the shelves.

"What's so funny?" she demanded, her pride apparently hurt.

He stepped into the small space and glanced about. "You need a sense of order," he said, trying to hold back a chuckle. "Put all the baking supplies together, all the tinned food, and so on. I promise you, it will be better in the long run."

She scowled. "How would you know?" she demanded as she glared at him. One thing Brody had learned, Claire was feisty. It was all he could do not to laugh out loud. He supposed she wouldn't like if he made fun of her.

He shrugged his shoulders. "I've seen what my mother and sisters do." He shrugged again. "If you don't want my advice, that's fine." He turned to leave, but hesitated for only a moment. Claire touched his shoulder, halting his departure.

"I'm sorry," she said quietly. "It's been a rather difficult day."

He knew exactly what she meant. Brody felt the same way. Instead of leaving her alone, he felt compelled to pull her into his arms and hold her tight. Wouldn't it be nice if holding each other meant all their troubles would melt away?

With his arms around his new bride, Brody felt better. It was almost like they had a connection. Except he knew that wasn't possible. And yet, in the short time they'd known each other, they'd already had an argument.

Over her dead grandparents no less. Joshua Foggarty jumped into his mind again. He would ask the sheriff. Perhaps he could shed some light on it. And if Claire's grandfather didn't inherit his riches, where did they come from? He needed those questions answered, otherwise they would niggle away at him and destroy his peace of mind.

One thing he knew for certain, and that was Claire had no idea about either of her grandparents. He would start reading Clarissa Foggarty's journal with her, and try to glean more information. It was the least he could do. There was obviously something important about that journal, otherwise, why would Claire keep it with her everywhere she went?

Her warmth against him made Brody want to stand like this all day. Claire's arms came up around his waist, and her head rested on his chest. They were getting far too cozy for Brody's liking.

"Claire," he said as he caressed her soft cheeks. "We shouldn't be doing this." He didn't want to stop, but knew they should.

Her eyes opened wide as she stared at him. "Why not? We're married." Suddenly, she looked terrified. "I…we really are married, aren't we? I haven't been tricked into believing we're married when we're not?" The last few words were barely audible as her voice became softer and softer the longer she spoke.

As much as he didn't want to remove his arms from around her, Brody reached into his pocket and handed her the folded paper the preacher had given him after their brief ceremony. "It's a bit crumpled, but here's the proof."

Claire stepped back from him and accepted the crushed sheet. Why she would think she'd been tricked into believing they were married, he didn't know. The more he got to know her, the more he believed something sinister was afoot.

Of course, that was his training kicking in. After a while as a lawman, you become suspicious of anyone and everyone. "Alright," she finally said after scrutinizing their marriage certificate as though her life depended on it. "I believe you."

Brody didn't know what to think. Something strange was occurring, and he meant to get to the bottom of it. "Let's finish packing the shelves in here, then we can make the bed," he said carefully. What his new wife would think about that, Brody wasn't sure. There was only one bed in the place, so they were stuck with each other.

Chapter Nine

"Joshua is always attentive and I love him dearly. Father despises him and says Joshua is hiding something. I fear he may be right."

Claire took a deep breath, then stepped into the bedroom she and Brody would share. Mother had never taken the time to talk to her about the intimacies of marriage, despite planning to marry her daughter off later in the year.

It wasn't as though there was a shortage of suitors—there were plenty. They seemed to come out of the woodwork the moment word got out the Foggarty's were ready to see their youngest daughter married.

Young, rich, gentleman began calling with a view to courting her. Claire shunned them all. They were boring. Most of them, anyway. She wanted someone a little more exciting. Money was everything to her parents. The groom's money that was. The plan was to join two wealthy families. They would never approve of Claire's choice of husband. If you could call it a choice.

A lowly deputy, soon-to-be sheriff would not suit their plans. Not at all.

She opened the packaging from the linen and flicked a sheet over the bed. Brody stood on the other side, waiting to help. From what she could see, they were both useless in that regard. "Haven't you ever made a bed before?" she asked, trepidation in her voice.

"Never. What about you?" Brody stared down at the crisp white sheets. Without waiting for an answer, he made a suggestion. "We could ask Mrs. Goodall to teach us? I've paid her until the weekend, so if we move in early, she will be jumping for joy."

Claire's heart thudded. Did he mean the boarding house owner didn't like her? "That came out wrong. What I meant was, she has already been paid, but you won't be there. She can rent the room out again. Double profit."

Nodding, Claire had another try with the sheets. It was then she noticed the pillowcases in the package. "We forgot the pillows," she said, now feeling defeated about the entire situation. "I don't want to be here, Brody. Something doesn't feel right." She glanced out of the window. People wandered around outside. Trouble was, she knew no one. Any one of those people could be here to harm her.

Several attempts had been made to remove the journal from her possession. At first, Claire hadn't understood it was her grandmother's journal they wanted. She still wasn't certain, but it seemed the obvious choice. Nothing else seemed to attract attention.

Even now, she wondered if it could be the simple fact she was an heiress. Many young women in her situation had been kidnapped for ransom. Many had been murdered before the ransom was paid.

"I…" Claire collapsed onto the side of the bed, and Brody came around to her side.

"Don't worry. I'm sure Mrs. Goodall…"

"It's not that," Claire said before he had a chance to finish. "I need to tell you something."

Brody reached for her hand, and immediately her fears seemed to lessen. "I'm listening," he whispered close to her ear. His warm breath on the side of her face was comforting, and Claire leaned into him.

"Someone has been following me." Claire heard Brody's intake of breath.

He turned to study her. "Has it happened since you arrived here?" He clasped her hand tighter than before. "Do you know who it is, what they want?"

Claire shook her head. "I don't know." She leaned into Brody, and his arms went up around her. It was far too convenient—he'd insinuated himself into her life at just the right time. Was Brody involved? She'd married the man, trusting what he said to be true.

She took another fortifying breath. What was wrong with her? People around town knew him, trusted him, and she needed to do the same.

"Unless…" She turned to face her new husband. "Could it be because I'm a Foggarty?" Claire felt vulnerable, but wasn't sure why.

"Because you're an heiress. Is that what you mean?" Brody reached out and touched her cheeks, then smiled. Claire felt heat rising in her face, and apparently Brody saw the effect.

"My parents have probably lost all hope by now. I didn't tell them I was leaving." She tried to blink away her tears, but it didn't work. Hot tears ran down her face. Brody wiped them away. "I can't tell them where I am. It will put them, and us, in danger."

Brody frowned. "The first thing we have to do is learn more about your grandfather. I have this niggling feeling in the back of my mind about him. Do you know if he was ever wanted by the law?"

Claire's breath caught in her throat. For a few seconds, she couldn't breathe. Was her deputy husband accusing her grandfather of being a…robber? Or an outlaw, or something equally terrible? "By all accounts, Joshua Foggarty was a gentleman. I can't imagine my dear grandmother marrying someone like that."

"She said he was a scoundrel," Brody said, repeating Claire's words of earlier. "In what way did she mean that?"

Claire blinked, trying to take it all in. "I'm sure she didn't believe he was an outlaw, or anything like that. I believe she referred to the times he pulled her close at the dance. They barely knew each other at the time."

It was clear by his expression Brody did not believe her. Instead of responding, he placed his arm around her shoulders. "We'll get to the bottom of this. If someone is harassing you, we need to find out who. More importantly, we need to know why. Do you feel up to going back to the mercantile for pillows? On second thought, we don't need them tonight. I want you to understand Bingarli is a good place to live. You'll see," Brody told her, then stood and pulled Claire to her feet.

He stared down into her face and licked his lips. Was he going to kiss her? Claire wasn't sure what she would do if he tried—she was innocent when it came to men.

"We should go," he said firmly, then pulled her out of the cottage. "I don't know about you, but I'm getting hungry. You won't want to miss your meal at the boarding house—Mrs. Goodall is a terrific cook."

Claire was sorely disappointed. She thought he might take her to the diner to celebrate, but she was wrong. Instead, they headed to the boarding house. After that, they would visit the mercantile.

It had certainly been a day of disappointments.

Chapter Ten

When he woke up this morning, Brody had not planned on getting married. He also hadn't planned on mourning his cousin. He and Earl had been close when they were younger. Never would he have predicted Earl would choose a path so different from Brody.

To be shot and killed right here in town made it even worse. For years, he'd told Earl he was putting the good folks of Bingarli in danger, but Earl wasn't convinced. Thankfully, no one was around when it happened, so no innocent lives were lost.

Now that he'd settled Claire into the boarding house for the night, he headed back home. He'd been there so long now, the men's boarding house felt like home. Walking into the sheriff's cottage with his bride today had been surreal. He realized now it must have been the same for Claire.

For them both, it had been a day of mixed blessings. Neither expected to marry the other, and neither believed the day would end the way it had.

Brody now regretted marrying Claire today. Had he known Sheriff Dodd had already vacated the sheriff's cottage, they could have waited a few days.

Scratching his head, Brody wondered if given time, Claire would have still married him. She may have decided him unworthy if she'd been forced to wait. And he may not have found out she was in danger.

His heart thudded. *Was she safe? Did her pursuer know his wife was now living in Bingarli?* It took all his effort not to burst into the women's boarding house and place himself outside her bedroom door. Brody knew exactly what Mrs. Goodall would think about that.

Instead, he forced himself forward and went home. The aroma of freshly baked bread enticed him inside. The other men were already seated around the table, about to say the blessing. Brody pulled his hat from his head. "Apologies," he said, then took his place at the table.

As hungry as he was, Brody wished he was anywhere but here. He didn't understand the reason behind it, but he preferred to be with Claire. The bride he barely knew.

Like most nights, the banter at the table was loud. Each man ate his fill while talking to the person sitting next to him. Brody didn't do that, and rarely spoke. He ate his meal, then left. He was the odd man out, all because he worked at the sheriff's office. It wasn't that he was shunned, but others were afraid to say something that might get them into trouble. It was quite the dilemma for many.

Still, Brody enjoyed living there. Mostly for the delicious meals.

He pondered life as a married man. With a wife who couldn't cook, and didn't know how to sew. Not to mention being pursued by a person or persons unknown. For a reason not yet clear.

"I hear you got married today," one of the men shouted across the table.

Brody glanced up at him. "You heard right," he said, then went back to his meal. He sensed the eyes of every man at that table. As much as he tried to ignore their gaze, he couldn't.

"What are you still doing here, then?" the man asked, pushing his point.

Carefully placing his cutlery across his plate, Brody glanced up. "Joseph," he said patiently, although he didn't feel that way, "I'm fixing up the sheriff's cottage. The moment it's ready, we'll move in."

"Heard she's pretty." Joseph waggled his eyebrows. Brody's patience was pushed to the limit.

"Shut your filthy mouth," Brody snarled, then began to stand. There was a reason he never spoke to these people. He came in, ate his fill, and went to his room. They all came from different backgrounds, but they were all the same. Their minds were in the gutter. It would not surprise

Brody one bit if he had to arrest any one of them in his role as sheriff.

The biggest surprise was he hadn't needed to do so already. They were drinking men and several were drunks. Keeping to himself had mostly worked, but not tonight.

Brody glared at the offending man, who backed down. His hands went up in front of himself, and he shut his mouth in record time. Brody sat back down and finished his meal. Except he had no intention of locking himself in his room tonight. Brody needed to get outside and into the fresh air, away from these vile creatures.

Brody pulled on his thick coat, pushed his hat on his head, and went outside. Even when it wasn't his turn to do nightly checks, he often did. Especially when he was restless, like tonight.

It wasn't pitch black, nothing like it. The moon shining high up in the sky lit up the town enough that he didn't need a lantern, which was the way he preferred it. Bingarli was a quiet place, and they rarely had criminal activity. Now and then they locked up a drunk, or someone was charged with theft, but it was rare.

The saloon was the town's biggest problem. A close eye was kept on the place. They had a couple of working girls there, but of their own choosing. If anything untoward ever happened, the sheriff would be right on it.

In a matter of days, Brody would be sheriff. The enormity of it suddenly hit Brody. He still didn't have a deputy, so between worrying about that and looking out for his bride, he had his work cut out.

He halted as he heard movement ahead. As he got closer, Brody discovered two men scuffling outside the saloon. "Break it up or spend the night in a cell," he called. They ran in two different directions.

If that was the most he had to deal with tonight, Brody would be ecstatic. He wandered around town checking out the stores, peering in the windows and ensuring the doors were locked. He'd been remiss today, and not done his deputy duties as he should have. There were more important things on his mind. Thankfully, Sheriff Dodd was sympathetic to his problems. Brody wandered toward the women's boarding house. Claire had been on his mind since he'd left her there earlier. First thing in the morning, he would quiz the sheriff about his wife's grandfather. The older man might recall something useful. "Except he's not old enough to have been around then," he mumbled. Still, he might have heard something. Anything would be helpful.

As he turned the corner, the silhouette of two men startled him. Brody's hand went to his gun. He moved stealthily toward them, not wanting to scare the pair off. "Turn around slowly," Brody demanded, his heart pounding. Were they looking for his wife?

The men put their hands in the air, and turned to face the deputy. His pent up breath left him, and anger took over. "What are you fools doing out here?" he asked, anger in his voice. "I told you both to go home or spend a night in the cells."

"Just watchin' the ladies," one of the drunks said. "Ain't they pretty?" A sly smile came to the man's face despite the fact he slurred his words.

Brody had heard enough. "You're both coming with me," he said, and marched them to the jail, but not without protests. The saloon seemed to attract the worst kind of customers. Brody rued the day it was built.

Then again, without it, he'd probably be without a job.

After he locked the drunkards up, Brody decided just to sit and rest for a while. A telegraph sat on his desk. He breathed a sigh of relief at the words. *Deputy Drake Jackson arriving end of week*, it said. It was the best news Brody had heard all day.

Chapter Eleven

"Joshua asked me to marry him. Father did not want to give his blessing, but knew we would marry regardless. Finally, he agreed, but only, he said, to ensure my happiness."

Claire watched as her new husband approached the two men who'd stood staring through the boarding house window. She'd been in the sitting room, chatting with some of the other women who lived there. Everyone was pleasant, and no one questioned why she was there, despite knowing she'd married the deputy earlier in the day.

She was certain Mrs. Goodall had explained the situation to them. For that, Claire was grateful.

The longer the men stood there simply staring, the more she was convinced they were there for her. Apart from worrying about her own safety, her biggest fear was putting other women in danger. Claire considered surrendering herself to her pursuers in order to keep the others from harm.

She was moments away from doing so when she noticed Brody come up behind them. The pair put their hands in the air and turned slowly. She watched them being taken toward the sheriff's office until they were out of sight.

Did that mean she was safe now? Brody wouldn't have arrested them for no reason, would he? Claire knew she couldn't assume anything. Until she was certain she was no longer being pursued, she needed to keep a low profile. Her husband had told her so. He also told her he would get to the bottom of the situation. Not that she knew him well, but Claire was certain if anyone could solve this problem, it would be Brody.

She had no idea what those people were after, unless it was Claire herself. It made her wonder what her father was prepared to pay if a ransom was demanded. She shuddered at the thought. The next few days would be crucial. Once she moved into the sheriff's cottage, Claire knew she would feel safer. Running the way she had recently was reckless and precarious. Forever on the move was not something Claire envisioned she would be doing. Nor did she ever believe she'd end up in a place that was but a speck on the map.

"You look tired, dear." Mrs. Goodall's voice brought Claire out of her thoughts. "Don't feel you must stay up. Everyone wanders off to bed whenever the urge takes them."

She glanced up at the older woman. "Thank you. I believe I will retire for the night. It's been a long day." Claire was grateful her room wasn't far from the sitting room, but it was far enough the chatter wouldn't keep her from sleep. She liked it here— everyone was lovely, friendly. If things had been different, Claire could see herself staying for a very long time.

Heading to her room and comfortable bed, Claire wondered what Brody was doing now. No doubt sitting at his desk filling out paperwork for his prisoners. She sighed. He would be exhausted. His day had been as difficult as hers, if not worse.

She barely knew the man, and yet she worried for him. What would she be like after they'd been married for some time?

Claire didn't want to think about it.

Her eyes fluttered open, and Claire couldn't believe it was morning already. She climbed out of bed and opened the curtains wide. The sun was high in the sky, and was shining brightly. She'd slept late. Claire sighed. More than likely she'd missed breakfast. Despite that, she was certain Mrs. Goodall would allow her a cup of tea.

After dressing as quickly as she could, Claire hurried to the kitchen. The aroma was delightful. Such a pity she'd missed out.

"Oh! Good morning, Claire," Mrs. Goodall said when she spotted Claire. "Come on in and make yourself comfortable." She turned away and poured a cup of tea for Claire, and another for herself. Next she added some muffins to a plate and pushed them close to her guest. "Your husband has already been around today. I guess he misses you." The other woman chuckled.

Claire resisted the urge to roll her eyes. He barely knew her, and she had to force herself not to state the fact. "I'm sorry. I don't normally sleep so late."

"You're excused," the older woman said, her expression one of compassion. "Yesterday must have taken a toll on you. So much happened, and in a short time too." Mrs. Goodall pushed the muffins closer. Likely because Claire hadn't touched them. "You need to keep up your strength, dear," she said.

It wasn't long before there was a knock at the door. Her hostess hurried to see who it was. Claire recognized Brody's voice. Already it was familiar, which felt strange to Claire. When he entered the kitchen, a shiver ran down her spine. She smiled briefly. Brody grinned. "Good morning," he said. "You must have been exhausted."

Claire's Regrettable Outcome

"Come in and sit down, Deputy," Mrs. Goodall said before Claire had a chance to answer, then directed Brody to the seat next to his wife. "I'll pour you a coffee." She turned away then, and Brody leaned in and kissed Claire's cheek. It was the last thing she expected. Still, she said nothing. He was entitled to kiss her since she was legally his wife.

Claire gulped her tea, then turned to Brody. "I saw you arrest those men last night. Is that the end of it?" She almost whispered the last words, hoping the boarding house owner wouldn't hear.

"The end of what?" Mrs. Goodall asked as she turned back with Brody's drink, her gaze piercing them both.

Without warning, Claire felt overcome with emotion. Brody covered her hand with his own. "It's confidential," Brody said, and Mrs. Goodall scowled. Claire nodded, giving him the go ahead to tell the other woman, but she could see he wasn't convinced. "I can only tell you if you keep it to yourself," he said firmly.

The shock on Mrs. Goodall's face was palpable. "I promise not to tell anyone," she said. "Are you alright, dear?"

"Claire has been followed recently, and harassed. We don't know who the perpetrator is."

Her hands flew to her mouth. "Oh my goodness! You are investigating, aren't you, Deputy Wilson?" Mrs. Goodall's hands slid down to her heart. "Of course you are. You're the last person to put your wife in harm's way."

Brody's gaze went from Mrs. Goodall to Claire. "To answer your question, Claire, that's not the end of it. I arrested two of the town drunks for watching through the window. They saw no issue with watching women late at night. I let them go earlier this morning."

Claire was far from reassured by the news. In fact, it was the opposite. She'd slept deeply last night believing her ordeal to be over. Tonight would be a completely different story. Brody's arm slipped up around her shoulders—his touch comforted Claire. She didn't want him to leave, but knew he must at some point.

"Some good news," Brody told the pair. "A replacement deputy is due to arrive by the end of the week."

"You must be pleased," the older woman said. "They certainly were cutting it fine."

Brody glanced at Claire before answering. "I admit to being extremely relieved. Although not the busiest town when it comes to criminal activity, the sheriff cannot work twenty-four hours a day. Until he settles in, I'll have to train the new deputy as well as do my job."

"At least you will have your wife to support you," Mrs. Goodall said, and Claire wondered what sort of help she would really be.

"Since I am officially Bingarli's sheriff starting tomorrow, I see no harm in us moving into the sheriff's cottage today." He studied Claire and she was certain he was trying to gauge her reaction to the news. "There are only a few things left to sort out."

This time, Claire did roll her eyes. "Like how to make the bed. We also need to buy blankets or a comforter." She watched Mrs. Goodall's surprised expression. No doubt at the revelation neither one of the newlyweds knew how to make the bed successfully. "I guess we'll be eating at the diner for a while, too."

"Drink and eat up," Mrs. Goodall said firmly. "Then we will all go to the cottage for a lesson in making beds. It's really not that hard." She scowled then. "Deputy, don't you make your bed each day?"

His cheeks went a bright pink. "I pull the bedding up each morning, if that's what you mean."

It was Mrs. Goodall's turn to roll her eyes. "All that is changing now that you're taking over the sheriff's cottage. It will do you both good, I'm sure."

Claire knew the boarding house owner was right. She was naïve to the ways of the world, especially those relating to being a wife. Since Brody was also inexperienced when it came to independent living, they would be learning together.

Claire wasn't sure how she felt about that.

Chapter Twelve

Brody watched carefully as they were shown repeatedly how to make the bed. He'd called into the mercantile and purchased a comforter and two pillows, then met the women at the cottage.

He admitted Claire would be the more likely of the pair to make the bed each day, as he often began work early.

"Now it's your turn, Claire." The older woman stood back after pulling the freshly made bed apart.

Brody noticed the color drain from his wife's face. "I can help," he said, wondering why she was so afraid of doing what was presented as an easy task. He shook himself mentally. Women make beds every day. It surely couldn't be that difficult.

"If you must," Mrs. Goodall said. "I do believe your wife is more than capable of this straightforward task."

"Let me try," Claire said, then began to flick the bottom sheet over the bed. After adjusting it to fit better, she tucked it in all the way around the bed, the way they'd been shown. Repeating the process on the top sheet, but turning it down at the top, she placed the comforter and pillows on the bed.

Then she stood back and studied her handiwork.

"You did well, Claire. Did you want to try, Deputy?" their tutor asked. "You never know when your wife may be indisposed."

Indisposed? What did Mrs. Goodall mean? "I suppose I could," he said, not believing for even a moment he needed to learn. Claire pulled the bed apart, and Brody attempted to put it back the same way his wife had done moments earlier.

He struggled to begin with, but with a little encouragement, Brody managed. It wasn't perfect, but at least now they both knew what had to be done.

"Wonderful," Mrs. Goodall said, slapping her hands together. "You have both done far better than I expected."

Brody pulled Claire to him and held her against himself. Pride filled him at both their accomplishments.

"Let's check the kitchen now, shall we?" the other woman said. Brody knew this would be a point of contention, since neither of them knew how to cook.

Mrs. Goodall went through the cupboards first. "You need cake tins and trays, and a few other essentials. No urgency though."

Brody glanced at Claire. She had gone bright red. As much as he wanted to, he couldn't stop her embarrassment at not knowing how to cook.

"Let's check the pantry now." They followed her into the small pantry, and watched as Mrs. Goodall assessed the contents. "You've done well. All the basics are there, except for dairy. I'm guessing you left that until you knew when you were moving in?"

"I…I don't know how to cook," Claire said hurriedly. Did she think her words wouldn't be heard?

Mrs. Goodall stared at her, then offered to teach Claire to cook, and the offer was greatly appreciated. Not only by Claire but also Brody.

They followed Mrs. Goodall from one room to the next, until everything was covered. She suggested a small number of items for the bathroom, such as soap. Brody made a mental note to get those later today.

"Thank you so much for all your help," Brody said, as they headed back toward the front door. "We both appreciate it." And he did. Brody knew without Mrs. Goodall's help, they would still be floundering.

The older woman headed back to her home. She had chores to do for her boarding house guests, as well as meals to prepare.

Closing the door behind her, Brody reached for his wife of less than twenty hours. "Well, what do you think?" he asked, pulling Claire to him. She didn't answer immediately and he wrapped her in his arms. "I know it's overwhelming, but things will get better. We can eat at the diner for now, and..." He was about to say, I'll help when I can. Only Brody knew that would be a lie. His work kept him away for long hours. As sheriff, it would only get worse.

Claire rested her head against his chest. "I'll do whatever I can to learn to cook. I'm sure Mrs. Goodall will be an excellent teacher."

Brody agreed. The woman was renowned for her cooking. Not only in Bingarli, but throughout the county. "Let's not worry about that now," he whispered, then kissed his wife on the cheek. He knew he was taking liberties, but they were married. Perhaps one day he might kiss her properly, and not feel guilty about doing so.

So much for wanting a marriage of convenience. He should have known better—Claire was a beautiful woman. Brody found himself wanting her more with every moment they were together. Perhaps they could make a real marriage yet. But first, he had to solve the mystery of who was chasing after her, and why.

~*~

"Joshua Foggarty… the name does seem to ring a bell," Sheriff Dodd said. "The family is from Helena, you say?" The sheriff scratched his head.

"Could simply be because they're rich?" Brody asked. He hoped for Claire's sake her grandfather had not been mixed up in anything untoward.

"Perhaps," the sheriff said non-committedly. "We may never know." He stood and went to the files that were housed behind the deputy's desk. Brody watched as his superior flicked through the files. Neither man said a word.

Brody made coffee for them both, placing a mug on the sheriff's desk. "I'm going to miss you," he said, meaning every word.

Sheriff Dodd turned around to face the younger man. "You won't miss me one iota. Now that you have a pretty little bride to distract you, I doubt you'll even notice I'm gone." He chuckled then, and went back to his search.

Without warning, he spun around with a file in his hand. Then he waved it in the air, catching Brody's attention. "Ever heard of Jasper Ford?" He shook his head then. "Probably not," he mumbled. "It was well before your time. Before mine too, but the case intrigued lawmen throughout the country."

Feeling as though he'd missed something, Brody reached for the file. "Not so fast, young fella," the sheriff told him. "I could be completely wrong about this."

"It's worth checking though?" Brody asked.

Sheriff Dodd nodded briefly. "More than likely, but come tomorrow morning, I won't be around to help you. Isn't your new deputy arriving in the morning? You could rope him in. Might be a good way to find out how experienced he is."

"That's the plan. Deputy Drake Jackson is supposed to be on tomorrow's stagecoach."

"Drake Jackson? Are you certain?" Sheriff Dodd asked. "I thought he was ensconced in..." He paused and waved a hand in front of himself. "I can't remember the name of the place, but he's been there for some years. Not sure what would have enticed him to leave his home town or his family."

The sheriff shook his head then drank down his coffee. "Not my problem. I'm sure he had his reasons. Maybe his wife left."

Brody lifted the mug to his lips and gulped it down. "I hope he hasn't brought his problems with him," Brody mumbled, more to himself than to the sheriff. Taking another mouthful of coffee, he braced himself for what he would potentially find in the file. With trepidation, he opened the file and started reading. The first thing he noticed was the outlaw's name—Jasper Ford. The person he wanted to know about was Joshua Foggarty.

It was at that very moment he understood why the sheriff had pulled that file and deemed it suspicious. Both names bore the same letters. JF. Except it proved nothing. Jasper Ford may or may not be an alias for Joshua Foggarty. The former was never caught, and the gold he'd stolen was never found.

If Brody knew criminals like he believed he did, Jasper Ford would not have acted alone. There would be a gang involved. The goods would have been shared—unless the mastermind of the crew took off with the lot.

Things were starting to come together. First, though, he needed to learn more about Joshua Foggarty. Claire might not like where this was going, but if she wanted to be safe, and Brody knew she did, he had to get to the bottom of this particular mystery.

Tonight he would start reading the journal—from the very beginning.

Chapter Thirteen

"The coming together of two prominent families was celebrated. Except by my father. He now hates Joshua with every fiber of his being. More than anything, he wants to see me happy. How can that happen without Father's blessing?"

As Claire read her grandmother's journal, Brody by her side, she became more and more distraught at her grandmother's words. Putting herself in Clarissa Foggarty's shoes, Claire understood the distress her father's hatred of Clarissa's choice of husband must have caused.

In fact, she could imagine what her own father would say about Claire's choice—if he knew. She wished she could get word to her parents about her marriage and whereabouts. Claire knew there was no way to do that without putting herself in danger. Perhaps even risking her parents' lives.

She wasn't prepared to do that.

"It sounds like the marriage wasn't happy," Brody said close to Claire's ear.

It made Claire wonder. "From what I've read so far, the problem was Grandmother's father, not Joshua." She turned to face him, and their lips almost met. Brody had been the perfect gentleman so far, and hadn't once taken any liberties. In some ways, Claire was pleased, but as a new bride, she wanted more.

Brody froze. Was it their lips being so close? Or was there another reason he paused? It could simply be he was mulling over her words. Brody had taken the time to read the earlier pages of the journal, while Claire had freshened up. She didn't know why, but something had changed. Brody seemed far more interested in the journal now, although he'd already taken an interest. Only not to this extent.

"Joshua Foggarty," Brody said as he caressed the back of her hand. "He seemed to appear out of nowhere. Does anyone know where he came from?"

Claire stared at him. Was Brody suggesting her grandfather was a...criminal? "What do you mean?" she snapped, instantly regretting her outburst. "I apologize," she said quickly. "I can see it appears suspicious, but surely my great-grandfather, with all his money and resources, would have checked him out?"

"If he did, your grandmother wasn't aware of it. At least not that she's written in her journal."

Brody was right. Not once had Grandmother mentioned her father had checked on her potential husband's background. Surely he would have done so? "Is there a way to find that out?" Claire asked, then wondered why she had.

Brody studied her for long moments. "That far back? I doubt it. There is no way to know if he had Joshua checked out." He frowned, then stared down at the journal. "The problem with journals is they are one-sided. We are only getting Clarissa's perspective. If only your great-grandfather had a journal. Now *that* would be interesting." Brody laughed, but to Claire, it was no laughing matter.

"Or my grandfather," she said tersely. "My grandmother left the journal to me for a reason. Perhaps because we didn't have a lot of time together. I'll never know the reason, unless it's further down along in the journal." She flicked through the pages, then went back to the page she was currently reading. Brody seemed far more interested than Claire expected he would be. "Mother never speaks of my grandfather," she said quietly. "It feels as though they had a falling out, but for what reason, I don't know."

"Maybe the journal will eventually tell us," Brody said, then took it out of her hands. "It's getting late," he said gently. "I have a big day tomorrow."

"Of course," Claire said, her heart pounding. Tonight was their official wedding night. She had no idea what to expect—such things were not discussed until a young woman was to marry. Then her mother would share the secrets of being a married woman. For Claire, though, that never happened as she'd had to run for her life.

Not that she knew what she was running from, or the reason why. With Brody's help, she hoped and prayed the answer would present itself. Sooner rather than later.

Brody stood and pulled Claire to her feet. Wrapping his arms around her, he held her tight. He stared down into her face, his eyes meeting hers. Then he studied her lips. "You're a beautiful woman, Claire," he whispered, then swooped down and kissed her thoroughly.

Before she knew what was happening, Brody lifted Claire from her feet and carried her to the bedroom. There he laid her on the bed, and began to slowly undress her.

Claire's heart pounded. He kissed her gently, and her heart fluttered. Soon she would know the secrets of married life.

~*~

Breakfast consisted of burned toast and coffee that was far too strong, but Brody didn't seem to mind. He pinned his shiny new sheriff's badge on his chest, then grinned. "I've worked hard to earn this badge," he mumbled. Claire believed he deserved better. A ceremony to announce his new position, perhaps? Except Brody told her everyone in town knew he'd been promoted. Besides, he *didn't like the fanfare of those pompous ceremonies*, to use his own words. It made her chuckle.

"The people in town love you," Claire said, proud to have married such a man. How would she have felt if she'd married Earl, then discovered his secret? As much as she wouldn't wish the man ill, the outcome had worked in her favor.

Brody gulped down the last of his coffee. "Not all of them," he said as he stood. "If you need me, I'm right next door."

Claire nodded. She knew exactly where to find her husband, if required.

"I suggest you stay here, and not let yourself be seen. We don't know who we're dealing with." He walked over to where Claire stood at the kitchen counter, preparing to wash up. She stared up into his face. Her husband was a handsome man, and a gentle man. Everything about him appealed to her.

He might have been coerced into marrying her, but she was so glad he had. Without him, she had no idea where she would be now.

Brody leaned down and kissed her lips. Then he wrapped her in his strong arms, and pulled her close. He might not love her, but at least he liked her enough to want to hold her like this. He pulled back, breathless. "I need to go," he said. "Otherwise I might change my mind." Brody pushed his hat onto his head, then turned back to face her. "My goodness," he whispered. "You are such a temptation." He kissed her again briefly, then hurried out the door.

Claire's heart fluttered. Never before had any man told her the things Brody said to her. Is this what being married was like? If it was, she would happily take it.

Chapter Fourteen

Brody scurried out the front door and toward the sheriff's office as quickly as he could. His wife was far too enticing for his liking. He might have started out believing they would have a marriage of convenience, but he quickly found himself being allured by her womanly wiles.

Not that Claire was trying to pull him in—far from it. She was innocent through and through. Except now she wasn't. He'd seen to that.

He groaned inwardly.

What had he done? Keeping everything at a friendly level and not getting personal was far better. Especially given he was investigating her grandfather. He was torn between wanting to discover who was chasing his wife, and learning more about Joshua Foggarty.

After reading part of the file belonging to Jasper Ford, he still had no clue as to whether the two men were one and the same. It made sense they were since, so far, he'd found no evidence of Joshua Foggarty's existence.

Still, he'd only begun his investigation late yesterday. Not even twenty-four hours ago. Far from it. He reached out and opened the door to the sheriff's office. Of course it was locked. He was the sole occupant for now. It made Brody wonder when his new deputy would arrive. Hopefully today, but the telegraph said he'd be here by the end of the week.

Before he'd even sat in the sheriff's chair, something Brody hadn't done before, the door opened.

"Good morning, Sheriff," Mrs. Goodall said. She held a mug of coffee in one hand, and a paper bag in the other. "How was breakfast?"

Brody knew she wasn't being unkind, but was worried for his welfare knowing his wife and her limitations. She placed the mug of coffee on his desk, and handed over the paper bag. It was warm.

"Two blueberry muffins," she said in way of explanation. "I thought you might be hungry." A smile danced on her lips, and Brody couldn't help but laugh.

"Thank you," he said, and truly meant it. "My wife's coffee was barely passable," he said, still chuckling. "And the toast was more like charcoal." He sighed. "At least she tried."

"Indeed. You eat up while they are still hot. I'll call back later for the mug so don't you worry yourself about it." She turned to leave, but turned back. "You

have far more important things to worry about."
Seconds later, she was gone.

Brody was grateful for the muffins. Black toast was
neither nourishing nor tasty. It didn't fill his belly
either. He bit into the first muffin—it was divine.
Brody knew he was being spoiled. He was also
aware if it wasn't for Claire, he wouldn't be
receiving this special treatment. Mrs. Goodall
seemed to have a soft spot for his wife. It had been
that way even before she discovered Claire was in
imminent danger.

After finishing the delicious muffins, he began to
sort the papers on the sheriff's desk. His desk. It was
difficult to acknowledge himself as sheriff, and
Brody knew it would take some getting used to the
title.

He moved his files across to his new desk, ensuring
the file on Jasper Ford was placed in the top drawer,
away from prying eyes. Why he did that, Brody
wasn't sure. No one ever came into the sheriff's
office to snoop, but you never knew. With each
passing day, he was more certain there was far more
to this case than anyone realized. Especially Claire.

He wanted to keep it that way.

After settling himself at the sheriff's desk, and
reassuring himself he was now entitled to that desk,
the door opened again.

A man in a deputy's uniform walked in.

Brody stood and extended his hand, coming around to the front of his desk as he did so. "Deputy Jackson, I presume?" he said, greeting his new deputy. "I'm Sheriff Brody Wilson." His new title sounded good to Brody's ears, but it would take a bit of getting used to.

"Everyone calls me Drake," the deputy told him. "I arrived a few minutes ago. Thought I'd check in here first." He glanced about the small sheriff's office, stretching his neck to see the cells.

"Nice to meet you, Drake," Brody told the other man. "Check out the cells if you like. We have no *guests* at the moment." The newcomer went into the area where the cells were, and returned shortly. "Why don't you get settled at the men's boarding house, then come back when you're ready. No hurry," Brody told him. "You've had a long trip."

"I appreciate that. I won't be long." He indicated the bag that stood at the door. "Not much to unpack. I travel light."

He was gone before Brody said another word. The new deputy seemed friendly enough, but Brody felt slightly uneasy. No idea why since they'd exchanged so few words and spent very little time together. He was in no hurry to make assumptions, and would see how things went over the next few days.

Not that it mattered. It was highly unlikely he'd be given a different deputy if he didn't like this one. Brody pulled the concealed file from the drawer, and began reading it. Nothing seemed to stand out as suspicious, but he would finish reading it, then give it to his new deputy. Between them, they might find something worth following up.

Brody drank down the last of his coffee, despite it now being lukewarm. Mrs. Goodall certainly made good coffee. He hoped she taught Claire how to replicate it.

Making notes as he read through the file on Jasper Ford, time passed quickly. It seemed like no time before Deputy Jackson returned. "That was quick," Brody told him, looking up from the file.

"Either that or you were involved in a difficult case."

Brody indicated the desk that was once his. "That's your desk," he said, stating the obvious. "Take a seat." Once Drake was seated, he told him the little he knew about the case. "The previous sheriff believes they are one and the same person," Brody said. "I'm not so sure."

"Would you like me to take a look at it?" the new deputy asked. "Looks like I have nothing else to do, anyway."

Brody handed over the file. "You'll find paper and pencils in the top drawer. Take your time." He stood then and stretched. "When you're ready, let me know and I'll give you a tour of the township."

Drake acknowledged his words with a nod, then began reading the file. His attention was all on the file. Even when Brody stood and moved about, his interest did not move from the papers in front of him.

While he waited for Drake's assessment, Brody read over his own notes. There was no way to compare this man, Jasper Ford, to Claire's grandfather. Even if they were one and the same, how could he prove it?

"Do we know the grandfather's date of birth?" Drake asked.

Brody stared at him. He mentally shook himself. "That's a good point. I'm not sure that we do. I can ask my wife, she may know."

It was the deputy's turn to stare. "Your wife?" The man was clearly confused.

"I apologize. I should have told you that from the beginning." He told the deputy everything he knew, including the fact the previous sheriff was convinced they were the same person. Even without any proof or evidence whatsoever.

After Brody showed the deputy where all the supplies were kept, the pair made coffee, then sat at their desks discussing the case. Brody still had a strange feeling about the man sitting opposite him, but couldn't fathom why.

Perhaps it was his aggressive approach. Especially since it was his first day working in Bingarli. Shrugging mentally, Brody realized Drake Jackson was likely aiming to give the new sheriff a good first impression.

"Let me get this right," the deputy said. "Your wife is being pursued for an unknown reason, by persons unknown. All she has in her possession is her grandmother's journal." He frowned and Brody knew the entire scenario seemed far-fetched.

It was then he realized it could all be a figment of Claire's imagination. It wasn't like he knew her well enough that he could categorically say her word could be taken as gospel. He took a long gulp of the awful liquid they called coffee. "When you put it like that," he said, not sure whether to say anything else.

As if reading his thoughts, Drake Jackson studied the sheriff. "I'm not accusing your wife of anything, so don't think I am," he said. "A telegraph message might clear up the question of whether it's the same person."

It was true. If Joshua Foggarty was who he said he was, they could disregard him as being an alias for Jasper Ford. "You're right, but it could take some time. Especially since we have no idea when Foggarty was born."

"Not even an estimate?"

Brody sighed. "So far, that information is not in the journal. If we come across it, we can do a comparison."

"Wouldn't it be quicker for one of us to read the journal? I'd be happy to take on the task," Deputy Jackson offered.

His heart pounding, Brody refused. "Claire won't let it out of her sight. It simply won't happen." He stood then. "I need fresh air. Let's take a stroll around town."

The deputy followed him outside. Brody still had an uneasy feeling about the deputy, despite there being no reason for him to feel that way. The only thing he could put it down to was the fact the man was new to town, and they were still getting to know each other.

He would give it a few days. Surely by then he would feel more comfortable in the man's presence.

Chapter Fifteen

"I was certain I'd be blissfully happy married to Joshua Foggarty. Unfortunately, I was wrong. He is gone more than he's home. Joshua is yet to say where he goes. It's difficult to admit, but it seems Father was right about him."

Claire heard her husband's voice, and hoped he was coming to visit. She glanced out the window, despite Brody telling her to keep away.

She knew he was concerned for her safety, but she was fed up, and becoming bored quite quickly. There was little for Claire to do stuck in the sheriff's cottage.

The knock at the door both frightened and excited her. It could be her husband, or it might be the person chasing her. Except if it was the latter, they wouldn't knock, would they?

"It's only me, dear." Mrs. Goodall's voice carried through the door.

Claire opened the door to be greeted with her new friend carrying an overladen basket, and her arms full of ingredients.

"What do you have there?" Claire asked as she ushered the older woman through the door. She carefully locked it as Brody had told her to do.

"We're making supper," she said. "All the ingredients you need are here." Mrs. Goodall put everything on the table, and began to sort them into groups. "We'll start with the meat," she said. "We'll need your biggest pot, and a board to chop up the meat. Oh, and a knife."

Claire knew they had to be there, because it was only the day before Mrs. Goodall had checked her cupboards to ensure the kitchen was well stocked with pots and pans.

"Today we start easy. You're making a beef stew for supper." She smiled at Claire. It didn't help with the terror she now felt.

"I…I can't cook," she almost screeched, scaring herself.

The older woman patted her hand. "Don't you worry. I'll be right here beside you the entire time."

Did that mean she expected Claire to do everything herself? Claire could barely hear herself think due to the pounding of her heart.

"First of all, put a spoonful of fat into the bottom of that large pot and sit it on the stove. We want it to get good and hot." Claire did as she was instructed. "Now, unwrap the beef and cut it into cubes, like this," she said, showing Claire what to do next. Then Mrs. Goodall stood back and watched as Claire tackled the task herself.

"It feels slimy," Claire told her, but continued regardless of the discomfort she felt.

She heard a chuckle. "You'll get used to it. Once you've cut all the meat, throw it into the pot. It's going to braise. After that, you'll turn it over and braise the other side."

Claire felt as though she was in over her head. None of it made sense. Never before had she stood in a kitchen, let alone cooked anything.

"While the meat is braising, you can start peeling and cutting the vegetables," Mrs. Goodall told her. "Cut the top and bottom from the carrots, like this. Once you've done that to all the carrots, rinse them. Now you can chop them up and put them aside." She stared over the top of the pot. "Time to turn the meat," she announced, handing Claire some kind of cooking utensil.

They'd done little so far, but already Claire's head was spinning. How much more was she expected to learn today? She wanted to be able to cook meals, she really did. Especially for Brody's sake, but

Claire had not one iota of what most deemed a good wife running through her veins. She simply wasn't brought up that way.

For her, it was more about learning how to walk without stooping, which colors worked best together, and how to act the way a lady of her status should. Not once when she was growing up did Claire believe she would need to know how to cook.

"Time to peel the potatoes," her companion told Claire. Then she stopped and stared at the new bride. "My dear girl," she said, patting Claire's hand. "There is nothing to be upset about. I will help you—we'll do it together."

Her words reassured Claire she was not expected to cook a meal by herself on her very first day in her new home. So much had changed over the past two days, including becoming a bride to a complete stranger, and sleeping in the same bed with that stranger.

It was all very overwhelming.

"Throw in the carrots, and then stir the contents of the pot. You'll need to add a few cups of water." Mrs. Goodall kept an eye on Claire as she prepared the potatoes. How she did that, Claire would never know. She cut onions next, along with a few other vegetables that Claire had no clue as to what they were. "These are ready to be added now," the older woman said. "Give them a stir. Looks like we need more water." Claire refilled the cup and poured it into the oversized pot. "The tricky part is not letting it dry out. You'll have to keep an eye on it throughout the day."

Claire did not like the sound of that. Putting her in charge of such a task was asking for trouble. "You can do it, I know you can. Let's start on the bread now." Shuddering at the thought, Claire nodded her agreement. "We'll clean up this mess first, to give ourselves space." Between them, the two women had the kitchen counter cleaned up and ready to use again in no time.

As she glanced into the pot, Claire decided she should stir it, so she did. "A little more water?" she asked her friend.

Mrs. Goodall smiled. "You're already learning. More water will definitely help. The water is needed to ensure the vegetables are cooking."

It was going to be a long day, Claire knew it was. She was determined to learn whatever Mrs. Goodall sent her way. The woman was gracious enough to help Claire, and she would do her best to listen and ensure her time was not wasted.

Not knowing when to expect Brody home was difficult. Mrs. Goodall had left once the stew was completed and cooking, and the bread ready to be put aside to prove. Despite not being experienced at cooking, Claire was proud of herself. She'd done well.

Even Mrs. Goodall said so. The kitchen had a glorious aroma about it, and she hoped Brody agreed. Whether the taste was up to his expectations was another thing altogether. The bread was now in the oven, and hopefully would still be warm when Brody arrived home.

She'd set the table, and tidied herself up, including brushing her hair and ensuring it was in place. Claire had also removed her apron. Mrs. Goodall said all these things were necessary for a good marriage.

There was so much Claire had to learn about being a good wife.

As the sheriff's wife, there was little for her to do except keep the house clean and tidy and cook meals. Unlike the preacher's wife who had far more to do, according to what she'd been told. For that, Claire was grateful. She was barely coping as it was.

Stirring the stew again to ensure it didn't stick, Claire heard the front door open. Then it clicked shut. Her heart fluttered. Brody was home.

Her new friend was right about the time she guessed Brody would arrive home. The bread was almost done, and would be ready to eat by the time they sat down for their meal.

"I'm home," Brody called as he headed toward the kitchen. "It sure smells good in here." By the time he reached the kitchen, Claire's heart was pounding—she was so excited to see her husband and tell him about her day.

It was there her thoughts paused. Mrs. Goodall told her the opposite—she should let her husband tell her about *his* day. It seemed strange, but the older woman had been married a long time before she became a widow, so Claire assumed she knew best.

Brody strode over to her and pulled Claire into a hug. With his arms around her, all her troubles seemed to melt away. He leaned back and stared down into her face. Then he kissed her. Her fluttering heart had Claire melting in his arms.

"Looks like you've been busy today," he said as he glanced across at the pot of stew.

Claire suddenly pulled out of his arms. "My bread!" she exclaimed, and reached for the kitchen towels to lift it out of the oven.

When she glanced at Brody, he was grinning. "I never thought I'd hear those words coming out of your mouth," he said as he chuckled. "Cooking lessons?" he asked as he grinned. "Either way, it smells delicious."

With the bread now cooling on the wooden board, Claire gave the stew a last stir.

"I'll go and freshen up, and be back soon," Brody told her.

Never in her life did she believe she could miss anyone so much. Not even when they were gone for only mere minutes.

Chapter Sixteen

As he washed up for supper, Brody pondered his feelings for Claire. Despite being deep into the case of Jasper Ford versus Joshua Foggarty, his thoughts turned to his wife throughout the day. The irony of it was, had Earl not been killed, Brody would still be a single man. He would have walked through that door as sheriff tonight, to an empty house, with no enticing aromas.

He would not have wrapped his wife in his arms and kissed her tenderly. It suddenly hit him how very lucky he was. A few days ago, he had not a care in the world. And no one to worry about, or to come home to. In the blink of an eye, his entire world had changed.

At first, Brody was resentful of taking on Earl's commitment. His feelings soon changed once he'd gotten to know Claire. His wife. The woman he barely knew, yet knew he was falling in love with. The pity of it all was she had no such feelings.

More likely than not, Claire had a suitor back home. Having to run the way she did left her no option— she needed to marry to change her identity. No doubt she was in love with the man she left behind. He was probably filthy rich too, unlike Brody who was far from wealthy.

Leaving the bathroom, he heard the clatter of plates in the kitchen. It made him smile. Coming home to his wife rather than the empty house he'd expected less than a week ago, was a far better option. He hoped that one day she would develop feelings for him.

Standing in the doorway to the kitchen, he watched Claire as she dished up their supper. She was beautiful. Far more beautiful than any woman he'd seen before. She wasn't the perfect wife, but then, who was? Outwardly, most wives appeared perfect, but Brody figured there had to be something they couldn't do.

Claire would learn, he was certain of it.

Her head shot up and she gasped. "You scared me," she said breathlessly.

Too late, he understood staring at her like that wasn't the best thing to do. She'd been chased and harassed by persons unknown to her, and for all she knew, it could have been one of them standing there. "I apologize," he said, then stepped toward her.

"Sit down," she said tersely, her face pale.

"Claire," he began, but she cut him off again.

"It's fine," she almost snapped, then straightened her shoulders. She stared at him momentarily. "Honestly, I'm fine. Sit down—supper is ready."

She took the wooden board with the bread to the table, along with a bread knife. A plate of butter already sat on the table.

Returning to the kitchen cupboard, she dished out a large serving of stew and placed it in front of Brody, then dished out a smaller serve for herself.

He leaned forward and breathed in the aroma. "It smells delicious," he said, meaning every word. "Did you make this yourself?"

Disappointment shrouded her face. "I did, with Mrs. Goodall's help and instructions." She reached across and took his hand. A shiver ran down his spine. Claire then said a blessing, and let go of his hand. Brody was shocked at the emptiness he felt.

He lifted his fork and took a mouthful. The food was hot and tasty. "This is excellent," he said between mouthfuls. Then he reached over and cut a few slices of the bread. Brody slathered it in butter, then took a bite. "Oh my," he moaned. "This bread is amazing."

Claire's disappointment changed to delight. She tucked into her food then, and Brody couldn't be happier.

~*~

Brody lay awake most of the night. Something bothered him about the new deputy, Drake Jackson, only he couldn't put his finger on what that was.

The man seemed efficient, and he was certainly helpful. He'd asked several times to see Clarissa Foggarty's journal, and was none too pleased when Brody rejected his request. After supper, he'd sat with Claire, and they read further into the journal.

Although her grandmother had initially painted a picture of a blissfully happy marriage, there were indications that all was not rosy between Joshua and Clarissa. Several times, she mentioned her husband disappeared for days on end. Clarissa voiced her concerns, but he'd waved them aside.

When she became pregnant, his *business trips*, as he'd finally labeled them, continued. Just not as often. It was clear Clarissa was concerned, but her reluctance to consult her father spoke volumes. She recognized her father had been right all along—Joshua Foggarty was not the man she thought she'd married.

Still, Clarissa continued to stay married to her husband, but her journal indicated she no longer trusted him.

Brody was more than a little intrigued now. He wanted to plough ahead and read more of Clarissa's journal while Claire slept. Except for the fact he'd promised he wouldn't, he would have done exactly that.

It was early morning, pre-dawn, and Brody was restless. Since he couldn't sleep, he might as well get up. Slipping quietly out of bed, he went into the kitchen to make himself coffee. It was then he noticed sounds coming from the sitting room. He hurried toward the noise.

A figure dressed in black was rummaging through the cupboard in there. What he was looking for Brody may never know.

"Put your hands up and turn around slowly," he demanded. Not only did the sinister figure not listen, he lunged at Brody. With no weapon on him, Brody had little way of defending himself, and landed flat on his back. He was a big man, but the attacker was even bigger.

The invader was quickly gone.

Brody stared after him. What on earth could anyone be after in the sheriff's cottage? The question baffled him as he sat at the kitchen table to drink his coffee while it was still hot.

"What's going on?" Claire asked, still half asleep. Brody stared at her disheveled hair and the sweet slumbrous look on her face. He had watched her sleep last night in his hours of awakeness, and decided he could watch her like that forever. In fact, he hoped he did.

He quickly stood and went to her side. "We had an unwanted visitor," Brody told her, then wrapped

Claire in his arms. She rested her head on his chest, and Brody was not unhappy.

"Did you catch them?" she asked, still not properly awake. "What did they want?" she added, then closed her eyes. How he lived without Claire in his life, Brody did not know. He now lived for every moment he got to spend with her.

He lifted his wife into his arms and carried her back to bed, pulling the covers up around her. When daylight came, he would investigate further. His questions were few—who would want to break into the sheriff's cottage, and what were they looking for?

Brody was certain he already knew the answer. If he was correct, how did that person know the journal was here?

Chapter Seventeen

"Joshua has left me alone yet again. With a little over a week to go before our child is born, Father is furious. If I were being honest, so am I."

Claire opened her eyes and reached out for her husband. Brody's side of the bed was stone cold. It was then she remembered getting up in the middle of the night after they'd had an intruder. She vaguely remembered being carried to bed, but that could have been a dream.

She hoped it was *all* a dream.

Hurrying out of bed, Claire pulled on her robe. Hoping Brody hadn't called the new deputy in to investigate with him, she headed toward the kitchen with trepidation. Surely if a stranger was there, he would have warned her.

Instead, she arrived in the kitchen to find him drinking coffee and eating leftover stew. "Good morning," she said quietly, so as not to startle him.

Brody turned to face her, a grin on his face. "Good morning," he said, then hurried toward her and wrapped Claire in his arms. "Did you sleep well?"

She stared up at him. "Was I dreaming, or did someone break in here last night?"

His arms held her tighter than before. "You weren't dreaming."

Claire gasped. Her mind went to the one thing of value in the cottage. "Did they get the journal?" Her eyes swam with tears, but she was determined not to let them fall.

"They left with nothing," Brody told her. "I think that journal holds information someone wants."

Claire's legs felt like they would no longer hold her. She pulled away from her husband and slipped down onto a nearby chair. "What sort of information? It's my grandmother's journal, for goodness sakes. By her own admission, she lived a boring life. Her husband and her family may have been rich, but she rarely left her home. Not to mention they had servants—there was little for her to do."

Her head in her hands, Claire fought the urge to weep. Why was this happening? How could a humble woman such as Clarissa Foggarty have written anything that would cause all this madness?

"Let me get you a cup of tea," Brody said as he stood. "There is something sinister about that journal, and I intend to get to the bottom of it."

Claire's head shot up. "Sinister? My grandmother was a wonderful person. She would never have been involved in anything like that," she said, not understanding what Brody was alluding to.

He placed a mug of tea in front of her. "I don't believe for one moment your grandmother was involved. From what I have read, she's completely innocent." Brody reached out and covered her hand. "It's your grandfather. I don't have the proof yet, but I believe Joshua Foggarty was involved in stealing large amounts of gold."

This was all too much for Claire. According to her grandmother, Joshua was loving and attentive. Except for the times he disappeared without explanation. Her heart thudded and her head spun. "It's why he disappeared for weeks at a time, wasn't it?"

"I'm afraid it could be. Right now, it's only assumption. With the help of my new deputy, I'm investigating." Then he gasped.

"What is it?" Claire asked urgently.

Brody stared at her. "I can't say. It's an idea that popped into my mind. Drink your tea, and do whatever it is you do." He stood then and turned to leave the room, but spun around to face her again. "Whatever you do, don't let anyone in except Mrs. Goodall, and myself. And don't leave here, no matter what."

Claire shuddered. "You're frightening me," she whispered.

Brody stepped over to her and kissed her forehead. "I'm sorry, but I need you to be aware of the danger." He hugged her briefly, then left.

Claire was in shock. She should never have begun reading that journal—it changed her life. And not for the better.

After Brody left, Claire sat at the kitchen table for several minutes. Brody's words echoed through her mind. Right at this moment she felt totally helpless. And useless. What was she to do if the same person broke in while Brody was away?

She ran into the bedroom and scrounged through the drawers. Claire already knew Brody would not leave weapons laying around, but she had hoped to find one. The kitchen! Perhaps she could arm herself with a large knife. Except she was more likely to harm herself than an attacker, and she knew it.

There was only one thing left she could do – and that was to scream at the top of her lungs. It was feeble, but the only thing she could think of to do if,

God forbid, she was attacked. Why would anyone want her grandmother's journal anyway?

Unless...

Could it be Clarissa Foggarty left some clue as to what Claire's grandfather had been up to? Why would anyone be interested in that information anyway? Shaking her head, Claire still couldn't understand why the journal was important to anyone except her.

One thing she did know, and that was the journal needed to be somewhere more secure. It had been in her bag since she left home, but since arriving at the sheriff's cottage, she'd left it in full view on the side table in the bedroom.

Hurrying into the bedroom, she came up with a plan. A weak one at best, but the journal needed to be hidden somewhere safe. Under the mattress perhaps? Except that was a common place to hide money or other valuables. It would be the first place anyone would look.

Claire's breath seemed to evaporate. If Brody hadn't tackled their late-night visitor, would he have entered the bedroom to secure the journal? Would the man have killed to ensure the journal was his?

Her heart pounded at the thought. Claire collapsed onto the side of the bed. She could no longer think straight, and the one thing she needed right now was a clear head.

She would dress, then make a fresh pot of tea and try to eat some breakfast. After that, she'd search for a far better place to hide the journal.

The worst thing she could have done was travel to Bingarli. Not only had she placed herself in a small town with nowhere to hide, she'd put others in danger as well. If something happened to any of them, especially Brody and Mrs. Goodall, Claire would never forgive herself.

Chapter Eighteen

Brody hurried out of the cottage, and was about to enter the sheriff's office. He needed to read through that file again—there was something he was missing. There had to be.

An idea had formed in his mind, but Brody tried desperately to brush it aside. Surely that couldn't be the case?

He shook his head, trying to clear his mind. Brody vowed to get to the bottom of the mystery. Joshua Foggarty came across as a good man. Until he didn't. What sort of husband disappears when his wife is about to give birth? And where is it he goes? If Brody could determine the where, he'd be able to discover the why, he was certain.

Except it was far too long ago. Claire's grandfather had died well before she was born. How would he determine what had happened decades ago? As it was, he was dealing with records that were incomplete. The file didn't mention whether Jasper Ford was ever caught, it just ended with him still being on the run. Then nothing.

That could mean the case was never solved. Alternatively, it may simply be the sheriff of the time was sloppy in his record-keeping.

As he leaned against the sheriff's cottage mulling it all over, Brody decided to start over. He would go over the file again, take fresh notes, and look at this as though it was Joshua Foggarty he was reading about. Then he would marry those notes up with the journal.

On the dates when the gold robberies occurred, was Foggarty at home with his wife, or had he disappeared again? Even to Brody it seemed like a crazy idea, but it was worth a shot. For now, he would keep it to himself. If his suspicions were true, it was best to do so.

He entered the sheriff's office with a new perspective and an open mind. "Any trouble overnight?" he asked his new deputy who sat at his desk drinking coffee.

"Nothing to report," he said, then stood. "I'll be off it that's alright," he said, and Brody nodded his agreement. Being alone would bring better concentration, and hopefully better outcomes.

He watched as his new deputy left. The man momentarily glanced towards the sheriff's cottage, then disappeared out of sight. Brody's list of tasks for the day were getting bigger, but he knew without them, he would never solve this mystery.

And unravel it he must.

~*~

He'd been at his desk for what seemed hours. Brody stood and stretched his arms and legs. As he did so, he noticed Mrs. Goodall heading this way. No doubt another cooking lesson for his wife.

Brody would not complain. Supper last night was delicious. The aroma that filled the cottage was amazing. He could certainly see himself going home to that each and every night.

He rubbed the back of his neck—he'd been sitting for far too long. Leaning over the desk reading the file and taking notes of dates and events was a tedious task, but had to be done. There was no way around it. Why he hadn't thought of this from the start, Brody didn't know.

The knock at the cottage door alerted him the food angel had arrived next door. Mrs. Goodall called out and informed Claire it was her. He wondered what the pair would be making today. No matter what it was, Brody knew it would be delicious.

He was grateful to the older woman. She'd really taken to Claire, even before she'd discovered the predicament his wife had found herself in.

The front door of the cottage closed, and Brody knew his mind had to return to the task at hand. He was about to sit down again when he noticed Sheriff Dodd heading his way. His back stiffened. How he would broach the subject he didn't know, but Brody needed answers and the only person he knew who could provide them was the former sheriff.

Brody stood beside his desk and waited for the older man to enter.

~*~

As he unlocked the cottage door, the enticing aroma hit him. "It's me, Claire," he called out, ensuring she wasn't startled.

He headed straight to the kitchen, assuming that was where she'd be. Brody was right. She turned to face him, a smile on her face.

"I hope you're ready for a treat," she said, stepping toward him, her arms outstretched.

Brody's heart fluttered. Good food and an affectionate wife—he could take that any day. As she reached him, Claire wrapped her arms around him and rested her head on his chest. He wondered if she could hear the pounding of his heart.

Never in his life had Brody believed he could be this happy. If fate hadn't stepped in, Earl would have been living this life. Obviously not in the sheriff's cottage, but in the little cottage he owned on the outskirts of town.

It was the first time since the brief funeral Brody had thought about Earl's possessions. That was a problem for another day. Right now, he would enjoy the arms of his wife. He stared down into her face. She seemed contented, and he wouldn't take that away from her.

Suddenly, Claire glanced up at him. "I'm so happy to see you," she whispered.

As he enveloped her in his arms, he leaned down and kissed her. Brody knew he'd been blessed the day Claire walked into his life, even if it was under difficult circumstances. "I'm pleased to see you, too," he said once he broke the kiss. "What is that glorious aroma?"

Claire smiled. It seemed to Brody it didn't take a lot to make her happy. "Chicken pot pie," she said, then turned toward the stove.

"I'll freshen up," he said, and headed toward the bathroom. Everywhere he went, he could smell the fruits of her labors with Mrs. Goodall.

What he didn't expect was to find a hidden treasure amongst the towels.

Chapter Nineteen

"Demanding Joshua announce where he was headed didn't help. I was convinced it was another woman, but Joshua vowed he loved only me."

Claire's heart broke for Clarissa. She couldn't imagine what she'd gone through with Joshua leaving every few months. Even more at times. His promise there was no other woman involved had not appeased his wife, and she poured her heart out in her journal.

It was clear Clarissa never meant for anyone else to read it. But then she'd left it to Claire in her will. It seemed like a strange thing to do.

Going by her words, Claire knew her grandmother was distraught, and the journal allowed her to get her feelings out. It was clear Clarissa's father had no time for Joshua, and that was a sticking point for his daughter.

At least now Clarissa had her baby, Velma, who would later become Claire's mother, to fill her days. It seemed even when he wasn't away, Joshua often isolated himself from his family. Knowing what Brody suspected, it was all beginning to make sense.

As they read the journal together, Claire pondered whether to continue. She could hand it over to Brody and let him read it alone. Except the journal drew her in. With each page read, Claire felt as though she knew her grandmother intimately. She wasn't the same woman Claire had met and loved. The woman in the journal was a shell of Clarissa Foggarty. It was as though Joshua's death had freed her from oppression. Had her grandfather been a cruel man?

Claire was beginning to believe he was.

Brody stared at her, then ran his thumb across her cheek. "It's heartbreaking, I know," he said gently. "I'm certain your grandmother wouldn't want you upset or broken-hearted for her." Brody pulled Claire closer to him and wrapped her in his arms. The journal had brought them closer together, and she was thankful for that.

Holding back a sob, Claire stared at him momentarily. "How can I not feel distraught reading her words? It's not some stranger I never met. Clarissa Foggarty was my flesh and blood grandmother whom I knew and loved for much of my life." Hot tears rolled down her face, and Claire had no control over them. Brody pulled her to his chest and held her tight while she sobbed.

When she finally stopped, Claire was exhausted. "I'm making tea," she announced, knowing it was one of the few things that brought her comfort when she was upset. "Would you like some?"

Brody shook his head. "I should, but no. I'd prefer coffee, if that's alright." Brody studied her, and Claire knew he had good reason to keep himself awake. And he would stay awake drinking coffee this late in the evening.

She hurried into the kitchen and made a pot of tea along with her husband's coffee. She was startled by a knock at the door. Her heart pounded—why would anyone come visiting at this hour? It wouldn't be much longer and it would be time for bed.

Claire hurried to the bathroom as Brody went to the door. He didn't appear worried, which made her believe this visit was pre-arranged.

Splashing cold water on her face, she heard muffled voices, both male. It made her wonder who their late-night visitor was. When she was satisfied her face was no longer red and blotchy, she headed toward the sitting room, where their visitor would surely be found.

The two men stood as she entered. "Sheriff Dodd," Claire said, surprised.

"It's plain Oscar now," the former sheriff told her. "You can forget the sheriff part. That's your husband's job now." He smiled briefly, and Claire knew it was only for her benefit. A quick glance at the two men proved things were strained, but she had no idea why.

"Coffee, Sh… Oscar?" she offered, and hurried into the kitchen without waiting for a response. Claire filled a plate with some pound cake Mrs. Goodall had made and gifted to her. While she was still learning to cook, it was a much appreciated offering.

She poured her tea to ensure it didn't become too strong, then made the coffee. She carried the coffee and cake into the sitting room on a wooden tray, and was about to leave when he spoke.

"Thank you, Claire," Oscar said as he reached for a piece of cake.

She felt Brody's eyes on her. "Claire," he said before she could leave them alone. "Oscar and I have business to discuss." She'd already assumed it would be the case, but was confused as to why they didn't go into the sheriff's office. "We need the journal."

The fact he didn't ask, and only gave her basic facts, told Claire there was far more to this meeting than Brody was letting on. "It's right there on the side table," she told him, then quietly left the room. Claire didn't ask questions—she was certain she would get no answers. Instead, she headed straight to the kitchen.

That tea sounded more enticing by the minute.

Oscar Dodd was still there well into the night. Claire worried for Brody—he needed his sleep. He always began work early in the morning, right after breakfast, and she hated to think how tired he would be.

She quietly went to bed after she'd drank down her tea. Their mutterings carried into the kitchen, but Claire couldn't make out the words. Nor did she want to. If two lawmen were working on the mystery of her grandfather's life, she would leave them alone. Brody told her the deputy had been reading the original file Oscar found, and wondered why they hadn't included him in this conversation.

Unless… She shook her head. Why would the new deputy be somehow involved? It made no sense. Except it was the only explanation she could come up with. Having covert meetings without the new man meant the two lawmen in her sitting room had concerns about him. Didn't it?

Claire knew it had to be true. And yet Brody had let him read through the sheriff's file on Jasper Ford. He'd told her Drake Jackson had requested to read the journal several times. He'd been quite persistent, according to her husband.

Was that what alerted him? What she couldn't understand was why the deputy would have any interest in her grandmother's journal.

Her heart pounded. Was he involved in the break in? Is that what made her husband suspect Deputy Jackson?

Her mind was racing, along with her heart. Claire laid back on the bed. She would rest her eyes, but had no intention of going to sleep. She wasn't even sure it was safe to be here in the sheriff's cottage, but with two lawmen in her sitting room, how could it not?

Chapter Twenty

The news from Oscar Dodd was not what he wanted to hear. But it was what he expected. The man who arrived calling himself Deputy Drake Johnson was a fraud.

Since the former sheriff had met the real Drake Johnson some years earlier, Brody had asked him to identify the newcomer as the genuine person. He now knew he was not.

The real Drake Johnson was described to him as short and overweight. The imposter was a little over six feet tall and thin. A man could lose weight, that was true, but growing at least five inches in adulthood—that was impossible.

They now worried for the real deputy's safety, and first thing in the morning, a telegraph would be sent to locate him. He would either be tied up somewhere remote, or laying dead in a field. Brody prayed it wasn't the latter.

Entering the sheriff's office on the premise of making sure he'd settled in was simple. The two men had chatted for around five minutes according to Oscar. The *deputy* couldn't get rid of him quick enough. That in itself was a giveaway. Being familiar with the real man was an added bonus.

Now the pair drank down their coffee, then began to read through the journal, tallying the dates of robberies against the departures of Joshua Foggarty. Every date so far was a match.

"We should continue," Brody said, "but I believe we already have our answer." He scratched his head for a moment. "Does that mean the journal will tell us where the gold is hidden?"

"More than likely," the older man said. "Whoever that is in there," he said, indicating the sheriff's office, "he believes it does. We should, too."

What a mess Claire had found herself in. Where would she be now if she hadn't arrived in town and married the sheriff? Brody didn't want to think about it. "More coffee?" Brody offered. They would both need it—hours of combing through the journal had taken its toll on the two men.

Both had worked through the night before. Instead of reading an old journal, they'd chased criminals. Even had shoot-outs. Those events were more to their liking. They knew what to expect. But a journal? This was new territory to both.

Still, Brody had to face whatever challenges surfaced. Oscar, on the other hand, was not obligated in any way.

After returning to the sitting room, Brody sat and sipped his coffee. Oscar did the same, but then held up a hand to Brody. He stopped and listened. At first he didn't hear it.

"The lantern," Oscar whispered, and Brody extinguished the light.

The quiet click of the door alerted them the intruder was inside the cottage. Brody prayed his wife slept and didn't walk into the middle of this disturbance. The moonlight coming from the open door showed him this man's height was the same as the fake Drake Jackson. He was thin like him too. Only this person wore all black, including his gloves and the covering over his face.

He closed the door quietly behind him, and headed toward the sitting room. The same place where Brody had accosted the intruder the night before. He was searching for the journal when Brody had discovered him, and was likely going to continue his exploration in the same area.

The two men sat quietly and didn't make a sound. Brody's heart hammered in his chest. He could barely hear himself think. He watched as their sinister guest creeped slowly into the room. Brody was impatient to pounce. Only, as an experienced lawman, Brody knew that was not the best plan of attack. They would wait until the man was close enough that he wouldn't get away.

It was one thing to believe the deputy was a fraud and had broken in the night before. Proving it was completely different.

With Oscar closer to the door, Brody waited for his signal. The pair had planned out their attack well before Claire had gone to bed. Their biggest fear was that she would step outside the bedroom at the wrong time.

At this moment, she was safely hidden in the bedroom. Brody quietly prayed she stayed there.

The man took several more steps toward the sitting room. The moment he was within reach, Oscar put one finger up. Brody prayed their intruder could not see them in the dark.

It was then they both pounced. The man was knocked to the floor, and the two men sat on top of him. The intruder growled and tried to get out of their grip.

The bedroom door suddenly opened and Claire stood there with a lantern. "Is everything alright?" she asked as she rubbed at her eyes. It was then she saw the two men on top of the trespasser.

"Stay there," Brody bellowed, and Claire stepped back. "No, don't go—we need the light," he said. This time, his voice wasn't full of fear for his wife. He cuffed the man, then stood him up. Brody pulled off the face covering. "Well, if it isn't the pretend Drake Jackson," he said.

"You!" Claire screeched. "How could you do this to me?"

~*~

With the intruder safely locked up in a jail cell, Brody hurried back to his wife. Oscar sat beside her when he returned, his hands full with a mug of coffee, and Claire's no doubt full with tea.

"Yours is over there." Oscar indicated to the side table closest to where Claire sat. Tears swam in her eyes, and more than anything, he longed to hold her.

Sitting next to his wife felt far more intimate than it should with Oscar in the room. Except Brody knew she needed to be comforted. An arm went up around her, almost automatically. He hadn't thought about it, and just did it. Never did Brody think he would act in such a way.

Even over such a short time, he'd come to really care for Claire. They might have been forced together by circumstances, but he now knew it had been for the best. For Brody at least. He had no clue as to how Claire felt. It broke his heart to think she may leave now the danger was over. Still, he would give her the comfort she needed while he could.

Oscar sat with the journal in his hands. He slowly turned the pages, reading the journal for further information. He must have become fed up with the slow progress he was making and turned to the back pages.

His eyes opened wide in astonishment as he read the words out loud, then flicked through the remaining pages. "There was a key here at some point," Oscar said, pointing to the faded outline of a key at the back of the book. "I wonder where it is now."

Brody glanced at Claire at the same time her hands went to her throat. "It…it was a gift from Grandmother," she said. "I didn't know the key was for anything. She said it was decorative."

The two men stared at her. "May I?" Brody asked, and at Claire's agreement undid the clasp on her necklace. "You didn't say who our prisoner is," Brody added, and Claire shook her head as though in despair.

"Lonnie Ford—grandfather's nephew. My cousin," she said. "Does that mean…?"

Things were finally coming together. "That your grandfather's brother was part of the gang? Most likely. Lonnie somehow knew about the gold and wanted it for himself." Claire sighed in relief. "It's over now," Brody assured her, and his wife sank against him.

Oscar took the necklace and placed the key on the journal over the outline of the original key. It fitted perfectly. Now all they needed to do was finish reading the journal and locate the gold.

Chapter Twenty-One

"The truth was finally revealed in a deathbed confession. Joshua Foggarty was not the man I believe him to be. He was a fraud and a gold robber. My heart hurt so badly, and at that moment I hated him for all he'd put me through."

Her grandmother's words broke Claire's heart. She couldn't imagine finding out like that, especially after all their years together. Clarissa's father was right—the man Grandmother had married was evil. After all Lonnie had done, it must run in the family. On the Ford side, at least.

As the front door opened, her heart was filled with joy. Anticipating Brody's return each day filled her with pure happiness. Except today, Claire awaited the news she prayed Brody would bring.

He had a smile on his face, but did that mean what she hoped?

"The real Drake Jackson is alive," he reported. "He is a little the worse for wear after being attacked and tied up by your cousin. The sheriff sent out a search party, and finally located him on the edge of town."

"Oh my goodness," Claire said, her heart pounding. "That poor man. It's something he will never forget. I feel so responsible for all of this."

"He's alive, Claire," Brody told her firmly. "Besides, none of this is your fault. He'll be here next week to take up the position he accepted. There are no hard feelings, and he bears no grudges toward you."

It still didn't sit well with Claire. The deputy could easily have died. Thankfully, he wasn't laying there, tied up for much longer—it could have been the end of him.

Claire stepped toward her husband. They'd not had much chance to get to know each other properly with everything else going on. Brody wrapped his arms around her and glanced down at her. Claire studied him—he was a handsome man, especially now worry lines didn't distort his face. She hadn't realized how stressed he'd been before.

Brody's head came down, and pushing her collar aside, he kissed her neck. "You smell nice," he whispered, no doubt catching the fragrance of the rose water she wore. As he worked his way up her neck to her lips, a shudder went through Claire. Since their unconventional marriage, she'd come to like and respect Brody.

No, that wasn't true. She'd come to love him. From the moment they met, Claire knew he was special. Not that she wished Earl dead, but she was glad his cousin agreed to marry her. From what Brody told her, life with Earl would not have been good. "Brody," she whispered as she pulled her lips away and leaned her head against his chest. "I have something I need to tell you."

She heard his heart beat faster. Glancing up, his happiness turned to sadness. "You're leaving," he said matter-of-factly.

"Leaving? Why would you think that?" she demanded, then went up on her tiptoes to reach his mouth. "On the contrary, I've fallen in love with you," she said, then kissed him thoroughly.

When she stepped back, the surprise was clear on her husband's face. "I love you, too, but thought you wouldn't be interested in someone like me."

Claire lightly punched his shoulder. "Of course I am. I can't imagine giving my heart to anyone else. Come on—supper is ready," Claire told him, and opened the oven. "I hope you like roast beef," she said, pulling the dish out of the oven. Her cooking was getting better with every passing day, and instruction from Mrs. Goodall.

"It smells delicious," Brody said. "Just like you."

~*~

Claire's Regrettable Outcome

Three months later…

With Lonnie Ford convicted and jailed, a huge weight lifted from Claire's shoulders. Her cousin was transported to one of the more rigorous jails, and would be there for some years to come. His greed had gotten the better of him, and once he found out about the journal, decided to pursue Claire.

It came out in the trial he wasn't certain the journal held the information he required, but he surmised it may be the case. Each of the Ford brothers were involved in the robberies, he told the judge, but Jasper Ford had stored the gold and wouldn't tell the others where it was. For decades, the gold was believed to be nothing more than a myth. And then Lonnie heard about the journal.

"What will happen now?" Claire asked her husband. "Did they find the gold? You gave them the information. Am I right?"

Brody pulled Claire closer as they lay in bed. "They did find it. We all assumed it would be in a cave or some secret location, with strong doors to stop others getting in."

"It wasn't?" Claire asked, confused by the information.

Her husband chuckled. "It was in a bank vault. Of all the places it could have been hidden, your grandfather chose somewhere inconspicuous. A place no one would look."

Claire sighed. "He might have been a scoundrel, and he certainly treated my grandmother poorly, but the man was clever." Brody's hand wrapped around her waist comforted Claire. She could not believe her grandfather had gotten away with all those gold robberies, and in the end, most of it sat in a bank vault untouched and unclaimed for decades.

"Don't discount how smart your grandmother was. She left clues all the way through that journal once she knew the truth. The only thing she didn't know," Brody told her, "was where the gold was stored. It took some time, but the marshals did their due diligence until they found the vault that fitted that key."

Silence fell between them, and Claire had something she wanted to say. "Brody," she said quietly. "There's something I want to tell you." She felt his entire body become rigid against her. "It's nothing terrible," she assured him.

Brody's arm came down and he rolled her gently to face him. "Should I be worried?" he asked, fear in his voice.

"Worried? No. Quite the contrary," Claire told him. "Brody Wilson," she said firmly. "You are going to be a father."

His grin was all the reassurance she needed.

Epilogue

Four years later…

Two-and-a-half-year-old Clarissa was inquisitive. She had to know everything that happened. She needed the ins and the outs, all her questions coming in fast succession. Right now, it was all about the horses. Brody had been teaching their daughter everything she needed to know. After all, she would help run their horse stud when she was old enough.

One-year-old Walter, named after Clarissa Foggarty's father, was barely walking, yet he was already enjoying his time on the pony Brody kept for the children to learn to ride.

He had quit his job as sheriff before their first born arrived. Earl's home had sat empty until his will was located. It was a surprise to both Claire and Brody that his property and all his possessions had been bequeathed to Brody. The reward Claire received for locating the long-lost gold helped to stock the large property with horses, and secured first their foreman, and later on, two more cowpokes.

The ranch was a thriving business.

"Do you think Earl knew what you'd do with this place?" Claire asked her husband as he led Walter around the front paddock.

"I do," Brody told her. "We talked about his dreams for the ranch often. The fact he brought it with blood money never sat well with me, but that was years ago. I imagine he is looking down now, a smirk on his face." Brody grinned. "He was like that, you know. Always smiling and joking around. It was one of the reasons he got away with…" It still hurt Brody's heart to think about his cousin's occupation, if you could call it that.

"Well," Claire told him gently. "We have been blessed. Not only did I end up with a wonderful husband who is the best father to my children, but we have a beautiful home, with plenty of spare rooms."

Brody's head spun to face her. "Are you saying…?" He lifted young Walter from the pony, and almost ran to his wife's side. Brody's hand went to her belly, then he leaned in and kissed Claire thoroughly. "I love you so much. And to think you were meant to marry Earl." The last words were filled with sadness.

Her heart broke at his words. "We've been blessed, Brody. Let's not think about what ifs. Let's live for today. We have each other, and our beautiful children." She rubbed a hand across her belly. "God had a plan for us, and it was always meant to be." Claire leaned in and kissed her husband as he held young Walter in his arms.

"Me hug," Clarissa called from beneath them. Handing Walter to Claire, Brody reached down and picked up their daughter. The four of them hugged until tears ran down Claire's face. All was right with the world. At least it was right with her family. God's plan for them had come to fruition, and Claire couldn't be happier.

From the Author

Thank you so much for reading my book – I hope you enjoyed it.

I would greatly appreciate you leaving a review where you purchased, even if it is only a one-liner. It helps to have my books more visible!

~*~

About the Author

Multi-published, award-winning and bestselling author Cheryl Wright, former secretary, debt collector, account manager, writing coach, and shopping tour hostess, loves reading.

She writes both historical and contemporary western romance, as well as romantic suspense.

She lives in Melbourne, Australia, and is married with two adult children and has six grandchildren, and twin great-grandchildren.

When she's not writing, she can be found in her craft room making greeting cards.

Website: *http://www.cheryl-wright.com/*

Facebook Reader Group:
https://www.facebook.com/groups/cherylwrightauthor/

Join My Newsletter:

https://cheryl-wright.com/newsletter/
(and receive a free book)

www.ingramcontent.com/pod-product-compliance
Lightning Source LLC
Chambersburg PA
CBHW070615120726
47909CB00004B/1230